The Man in Room Number Four

By: Rodney Riesel

ISBN: 978-0-9894877-2-6

Published by Island Holiday Publishing

East Greenbush, NY

Special thanks to:

Leon & Chris Frost

at

Bellinger Rose Bed & Breakfast

Cover Design by:

Connie Fitsik

To learn about my other books friend me at

https://www.facebook.com/rodneyriesel

For Brenda,
Kayleigh, Ethan,
& Peyton

Chapter One

Claire Dunning shuffled her bare feet along the old oak floor as she made her way down the hall to the foyer. The hardwood was cold this time of the year, especially in the evening after the sun sunk into the horizon. Wearing jeans, a white t-shirt, and a man's gray cardigan that was at least three sizes too big for her, Claire wondered where her house slippers were. She remembered wearing them when she came down this morning. *Maybe I left them in the bathroom*, she thought.

As she walked past the parlor she glanced in and saw Mr. Phillips sitting in the large, plush, red chair that faced the fireplace. The stained glass swag light that hung above him from an antique brass chain caused a glare that shined through his black comb-over. His legs were crossed, and the book he was reading lay balanced on his knee. Claire's eyes shifted to the empty slot on the bookshelf. She speculated which book he had chosen. Mr. Phillips turned his head and peered over the top of his thick-rimmed reading glasses when he heard the floor squeak, as she walked by, then he smiled and Claire returned the grin.

Robert Phillips was in town on business, that's what he said when he signed the guest book the morning before, and when he had signed the guestbook about once every six months for the past three years. He would always stay for about a week during each visit, hitting every hotel, motel, bed and breakfast, nursing home, and pharmacy within thirty miles, and then move on to the next town. Claire often wondered if he always stayed in the same places when he visited those towns as well, or if he just really liked her bed and breakfast.

Bob appeared every bit his age, late fifties, give or take. His stature was impressive at about six and a half feet tall. Claire had never seen him without a three-piece suit or at least a button up shirt and sport coat, and if he wasn't working, he was reading. He would read just about anything and often brought his own books, most times leaving them in the bookcase for future guests. His giant hands made the books he held look like toys, and the floors of the old bed and breakfast creaked underneath his step wherever he walked. He wasn't a fat man, just big, and Claire liked it when he stayed at the bed and breakfast. It made her feel safe having him around.

Bob sold grab bars up and down the east coast. Not just any grab bar, mind you. These grab bars, you see, were made from a new, light-weight alloy. Evidently it was the same type of alloy used in making the landing gear of space shuttles. That, combined with the state-of-the-art mounting system that allowed for a quick ten-minute installation, that even a child could handle, made it the number one grab bar in the United States.

The first time Claire heard the spiel, she wondered if anyone would possibly fall for it. Two years later, after buying nine of them for her own bed and breakfast, she was still wondering how *she* had. Luckily for Claire, Bob had no bridges to sell.

The front door was open and she glanced out past the front porch and into the cool, dark night as she grabbed the oak newel post, rounded the corner, and made her way up the stairs in search of her missing slippers. The bottoms of her feet welcomed the warmth of the carpeted steps.

At the top of the stairs and to the right was a bedroom door, and on the door was a number three made of polished brass. Claire put the palm of her left hand on the wobbly newel post as she reached the top step and turned to walk down the long hallway that led to her and her son's bedrooms. She walked past room number four and then five before reaching her son's bedroom door. She knocked before entering.

Mica was lying, stomach down, on his bed with his math book opened. He scribbled numbers and equations into a spiral notebook with his yellow number two pencil. He turned the pencil over to use the eraser and then remembered he had chewed it off.

"Why don't you do your homework at your desk?" Claire asked, motioning toward the small wooden desk and chair set in the far corner of the room.

"I dunno," Mica answered, never looking up from his work.

"Are you almost finished with your homework?"

Mica counted how many problems he had left to do, pointing at each one with his index finger. "Eight more."

Mica was ten years old but in some ways acted much older. It had been a little over two years since his father, lying in a hospital bed, told him that soon *he* would be the man of the house.

"Son, make sure you take care of your mom," he had said.

Two weeks later Mica sat next to his mother in a metal folding chair at his father's graveside. He tried to be strong for his mother, like his father had told him, but he couldn't stop the tears from streaming down his pink cheeks. Eventually the tears stopped and Mica faced the world a different boy.

"When you're done, jump in the bath and then you can watch TV for an hour before bed."

"Okay, Mom." Mica smiled his consent.

Claire carefully shut Mica's door, lifting the knob of the old wooden door just enough to get it to click into the right spot, and then she pivoted and walked across the hall to her own bedroom. Quietly opening the door, she stepped inside. After closing the door behind her, she leaned back against it. With her eyes shut and still clutching the doorknob she let her head fall back against the door and took a deep breath through her nose, then exhaled slowly through her mouth.

When she opened her eyes she found herself staring into the full-length, wooden floor mirror that sat directly across the room from her. With her elbows she pushed herself away from the door and ambled across the beige carpet toward the mirror, never losing eye contact with herself. Once standing two feet from the mirror, she stopped but continued to stare. She inspected the tiny crow's feet around her eyes. Taking the thumb and finger from each hand, she placed them alongside both eyes and stretched the skin, making the laugh lines disappear. She let go and they instantly reappeared. She sighed defeated.

Claire's eyes shifted to her breasts and she pulled open the cardigan. She wore no bra, and the cool night air hardened her nipples as they pushed against the thin cotton t-shirt. Her breasts weren't large but by no means small.

"More than a handful is a waste," her husband once joked. With her right hand she placed it against her shirt and under her left breast and lifted. She watched as she let go, letting it fall back into place.

Her husband's voice echoed in her head. "You're beautiful," he would always tell her when she complained about a new wrinkle or mentioned the fact that her bottom or breasts weren't as perky as they once were. Claire's husband, Clay, would say things like, "Why are you worrying about aging? You should be grateful that you look better than most women half your age."

When Clay would say these things to her, he wasn't just saying them to be nice; he was being honest. Claire *was* beautiful; she was just one of those women who never seemed to believe it, no matter how hard her husband had tried to convince her. Other men often stared at her, but she would convince herself that those men would stare at anyone who breathed.

Claire closed her cardigan and buttoned three of the six buttons. She glanced toward the two windows in her room that faced the front street. The blinds were open and she had a slight feeling of embarrassment as she wondered if anyone had seen her through the window making her bodily inspections. Walking over to the windows, she shut the blinds, hoping no one was lurking in the shadows.

Chapter Two

At 5:30 a.m. the clock radio on the nightstand began playing "Tupelo Honey." Claire rolled over and in one swift motion she smacked the snooze button with the palm of her hand. Pavlov would have been proud. Nine minutes later, when the alarm went off for the second time, Dunquin Cove's only radio station was just finishing playing "Fire and Rain." Claire squinted and tried to focus her eyes on the time display to see if nine minutes had really gone by in what felt like thirty seconds. She thought about hitting the snooze button again, but her mind had already started making a mental list of everything that had to be done that day, number one being preparing breakfast for the three guests.

Claire rolled onto her back and laid under the puffy, white, goose down comforter staring up at a small crack in the plaster ceiling. She wondered if the crack would spread. Then another thought struck her. Should she patch the crack? And then another thought... just how exactly *do* you patch a crack?

After "Fire and Rain" was a commercial for Freddie's Lobster Shack, the freshest lobster in Maine, then a sales pitch for Dunquin Auto Sales, and finally 104.2's very own Big Larry Lincoln announced the days weather.

Claire threw back the comforter, swung her feet over to the floor, and switched off the radio. Bending over and grabbing her red-and-green-checkered, flannel pajama bottoms, she pulled them on and made her way to her bathroom.

*****

Thirty minutes later she headed down stairs.

"Good morning, Claire," Bob Phillips said as she walked through the dining room to the kitchen. Bob sat in one of the eight chairs at the large oak dining room table reading the Dunquin Crier he had retrieved from the front porch only moments earlier.

"Good morning, Mr. Phillips," Claire responded with a half-smile.

"Mr. Phillips," he chuckled. "That was my dad's name, Claire. You know, I've been staying here off and on for over three years now. I think you can start calling me Bob." He waited for a reply but didn't get one. Instead he heard the familiar sounds of pots, pans, and chafing dish lids being pulled from the cupboards.

Bob resumed reading his paper. He didn't have to look up again to know what Claire was doing. He had seen her morning ritual for years now and could predict every step. First she would walk back into the dining room with two, two-quart containers full of hot water, followed by her distributing the contents between the four chafing dishes that sat on a table against the wall between the patio door and the dining room window. Claire would then walk back to the kitchen and return a few seconds later with four lids and set one on each chafing dish. She would open a hidden drawer under the table and pull out four cans of Sterno fuel, place one under each dish, and light them with a disposable lighter that she kept in the pocket of her apron.

"Can I give you a hand?" Bob offered, just like he did almost every morning.

"No thanks," Claire replied, just like always, before returning to the kitchen to start preparing the breakfast.

This morning breakfast would be scrambled eggs, bacon, sausage links, potatoes, and a few pancakes that were left over from the morning before.

"Looks like it's going to be a nice day," Bob said.

"That's what they're saying," Claire replied.

Claire scooped the eggs, potatoes, and pancakes into chafing dishes of their own and the bacon and sausage shared a dish, each in their own half-pan. She placed a small, white dish in front of each item and on them she set large spoons or tongs, depending on which utensil was suited for what item. She then set an open loaf of white bread next to the toaster that sat on the same table. She returned to the kitchen to retrieve the last few items that would complete the buffet set up; a container of milk, maple syrup, a small basket containing butter pads, and two carafes filled with hot coffee, one regular and one decaf.

"Unseasonably warm for the next few days," Bob added.

Claire grinned at Bobs attempt to sound like a weatherman. "That'll be nice for a change."

When the buffet table was complete, Claire turned her attention to the dining room table. She set a place for herself, Mica, and each of her three guests.

"Help yourself Mr. Phil— Bob. I better get Mica up for school."

Claire reached behind her back, untied the apron, pulled it off over her head, and hung it on the door knob of the door that led from the dining room to a small slate patio on the side of the house.

As Claire arrived at the top of the stairs, the door to room number three opened. Mrs. Owens was startled to see Claire as she exited her room.

"Oh, good morning, Claire," said Mrs. Owens, her hand rising to touch her chest.

"Good morning," Claire answered. "Sorry, I didn't mean to scare you."

"That's okay dear."

"Breakfast is ready when you and Mr. Owens are," Claire called back over her shoulder as she made her way to Mica's bedroom door.

Claire gave the door two quick knocks and entered. "Mica."

A muffled groan came from beneath the covers. Claire put her hand on her son's back and shook him, then pulled the blanket off of his head. "Come on, Mica; time to get up for school."

Mica pulled his pillow over his head. "Ugh, a few more minutes."

Claire shook him again. "Come on, breakfast is ready. Let's get moving." As she was leaving his room she gave him one more "Come on," then went to her own room to get dressed.

Already it felt like a long day, yet it was only the beginning.

Chapter Three

It was the cry of a seagull that awakened him. He lay on his back looking up through the tall grass at the clouds slowly moving by. The seagull screeched again and he turned his head to see two of them fighting over a small bag of Doritos. Something flashed in his brain. *Grab me a Dr. Pepper and a little bag of Doritos*.

One of the gulls grabbed the bag away from the other and tried to fly off but the bag was too heavy.

His nose was running, so he sniffed and winced in pain. He wiped at his nose with the back of his hand and examined it. Blood. His head hurt. He tried to shift his body into a more comfortable position. "Ahh!" he cried. *What if I'm paralyzed*, he thought. The gulls continued to argue over the bag of chips. *Is this a dream?*

Lifting his head slightly, he eyed his feet, and one at a time wiggled each foot and breathed a sigh of relief. Then he made a fist with each hand and opened them, stretching his fingers.

So far so good.

Feeling the ground for something to throw at the birds, his fingers found a small clump of dirt that he picked up and threw. The birds pretended not to notice.

I gotta get up. He tried to roll over again, this time making it to his side. He lay there a moment and then rolled the rest of the way to his stomach. He heard the sound of a car engine approaching. *I must be near a road.* He lay still, wondering if he should be hiding or if he should be making his way toward the road for help. The sound of the car faded as it passed by and kept going into the distance.

He put the palms of his hands against the dirt and pushed himself to his knees. Even on his knees the grass swayed above his head. He slowly rose to his feet, and the gulls flew off without their snack.

He was standing in the middle of a field. Fifty yards in front of him was a wooded area. To his left and right were more trees. He turned around, and twenty yards behind him another car drove by. He started to raise his hand but stopped himself. *Where am I?*

Reaching down he picked up the bag of Doritos and inspected it. He opened it and jammed his hand into the bag, pulling out a fistful of chips and stuffing them into his mouth. His jaw hurt to chew but he was hungry. *How long has it been since I ate?* He limped toward the road.

When he came to a grassy ditch at the edge of the roadside, he tried to jump over it but instead stumbled and landed in the dirt on his hands and knees. *God dammit!* Staying on his hands and knees for a moment, he stared at the ground beneath him, where the earth met the blacktop. There were small bits of red plastic. He picked up a piece and examined it. *Broken tail light?* He lifted his head and looked around. There were more broken pieces of plastic and glass scattered about.

After tenderly rising back to his feet, he looked in one direction and then the other. A few feet away and to his right, a sign at the edge of the road read; DUNQUIN COVE, 2 MILES.

Chapter Four

"Come on, Mica. Finish up your breakfast, the bus will be here any minute," Claire called out to her son.

Mica sat at the table across from Mr. and Mrs. Owens. Mr. Owens, sipping his coffee, peered over the top of the mug. "Ya better get movin', mister," he said with a wink.

Mica looked up from his scrambled eggs with a grin. "I know, I know." He grabbed his glass of milk and took one last gulp, got up, and headed for the front door.

"Is that your backpack on the floor, sweetie?" Mrs. Owens asked, pointing at the backpack Mica had just jumped over.

Mica turned and grabbed the pack full of books. "Thanks, Ma'am."

Bob Phillips flipped the newspaper to the next page. "Boy would forget his head if it wasn't attached."

Cam Owens chuckled.

On his way out, Mica grabbed his jacket off of the hallway closet doorknob. His mother puckered her lips to kiss him goodbye as he ran past, but Mica dodged the kiss. He was too old for that, and what if one of his friends on the school bus saw? He would surly get picked on during the entire ride to school. He already had to put up with ribbing from the older boys on the bus who referred to his mom as "hot mom."

Claire made a smacking sound as Mica flew by and called out after him, "I love you. Have a nice day." He would always be her little boy no matter how old he *thought* he was. Mica ignored his mother's well wishes and climbed aboard the school bus. Claire watched through the school bus windows as he ambled down the aisle and found his seat. As the bus pulled away, Mica glanced through the glass and gave his mother a quick half-grin.

Claire let the door slam shut, then stood for a moment staring through the screen at the giant maple tree in the front yard. Most of the leaves had fallen, and she had put off raking them into piles longer than she should have. She decided that today was the day. Turning to face the lingering chores waiting for her inside, Claire made her way down the hall back to the dining room to clear the breakfast dishes, and after that she'd clean the kitchen.

"Can I give you a hand, dear?" Mildred Owens asked as she watched Claire clear the table.

Claire chuckled. "Mrs. Owens, you're a guest here. How would that look if I put you to work?"

"I know, dear, I just feel a little foolish sitting here doing nothing while you clean up."

The smile still on her face, Claire responded, "It's my job, Mrs. Owens. If I didn't enjoy it, I wouldn't do it."

"Okay, okay, but please, dear, call me Mildred, and if you do need any help with anything, don't hesitate to ask."

"For chrissakes, Mildred, let the woman do her job and quit bugging her," Cam Owens chided as he leaned back in his chair rubbing his almost non-existent belly. "If you want to make yourself useful, jump up and grab me another cup-a-joe."

Mildred gave Claire a wink. "Sorry, I'm retired, Cam."

"That's what I thought."

Cam Owens was lanky, towering a foot and a half over his diminutive wife Mildred. His knobby arms and boney fingers hung almost to his knees. His skin was dark and his face ran deep with wrinkles brought on from years of working in the sun. He wore an old John Deere hat that he always tipped when meeting a lady, or hung from his knee while sitting at the table. Cam was a Levis man, sometimes they were blue and sometimes they were tan, but they were always Levis. Today his shirt of choice was a long-sleeved western cut shirt with pearl snaps.

Cam and Mildred were in their early seventies and had recently sold their ranch in the Oklahoma panhandle. Mildred had always wanted to travel, but until last year she had only ventured outside of Cimarron County on one occasion for a trip to the Oklahoma State Fair. Cam had always told her that someday they would travel the country, and two months after the ranch sold they hit the road.

Mildred always wore a smile on her face. Claire thought she looked like a cross between Mrs. Claus and Grandma Walton. One look at her and you just knew that if you got too close, she probably smelled like Toll House cookies. Mildred wore brand new white Sketcher sneakers and often looked down at them while she walked, the way one would look at the reflection of his new car in a passing store window as he drove by. It was obvious that she had never worn a pair of sneakers in her life until she retired, and she was really enjoying them.

Claire finished stacking the dishes, picked them up, and disappeared through the kitchen door.

Chapter Five

He stopped and stared at the large, green, wooden sign. The white letters read;

WELCOME TO DUNQUIN COVE

POPULATION: 3,842

SETTLED IN 1681

Dunquin Cove? He wondered. *Where in the hell is Dunquin Cove?*

He stumbled around the sign, using it to steady himself as he passed it, and continued down the road. After wiping a bead of sweat from his brow, he tried to shade his eyes from the sun. His head hurt and an annoying ringing irritated his ears. He rubbed his hands along his aching ribs as he staggered.

Continuing his journey, he glanced across the street and noticed there was now a sidewalk. *Must be getting close to something*, he thought. He crossed to the other side and began following the sidewalk's path. A white street sign on a black pole told him he was on Shore Drive. He came to a white picket fence and behind it was a large Victorian home with elaborate moldings and trim work. His head pounded with every beat of his heart, and as he wobbled, it felt like the sidewalk was moving. *I gotta lie down.*

He passed a few more houses and a few more fences until he came to another impressive Victorian behind a three-foot cast-iron fence. A sign in the front yard read, THE COLSOME HOUSE, BED AND BREAKFAST.

He stared at the beautiful woman in the front yard raking leaves. She slowly turned in a circle as she raked the leaves into a neat pile. He swayed as everything continued to spin, and he reached out to steady himself against the chill of the metal fence. A breeze blew the hair away from her face and he caught her watching him out of the corner of her eye. She stopped raking as she turned her head to look at him.

"Can I help you?" she asked.

He stood silently not knowing what to say.

She eyed her front door, and then returned her gaze back to the stranger. Noticing his ripped pants and the blood on his face, she asked, "Are you okay?"

He rested his hand on the lump on his forehead. "I need help." He reached over and unlatched the gate.

Claire dropped the rake and backed up toward the house.

"Please," he pleaded, opening the gate. He reached out his hand to her.

Claire slowly backed further away as the man continued toward her. His ankle twisted at the edge of the walkway and he stumbled to his knees. Claire froze as he knelt on the ground.

"I'm hurt." His voice was faint, almost a whisper.

He fell to his side and she ran to him. Putting her hands under his arms she tried to lift him, but he was too heavy. Claire heard the screen door slam behind her, it was Bob Phillips.

"Bob, help me," she called out. "He's hurt."

Bob ran to her side. "Who is he?"

"I have no idea. Let's get him inside and call 911."

The stranger opened his eyes and looked at Claire, squeezing her arm tightly. "No … no cops … please, no cops." as he exhaled his last word his eyes rolled back and his head fell into Claire's lap.

Chapter Six

Claire, Bob, and Mildred stood at the foot of the queen-sized bed in room number four, an unlit, polished brass chandelier hung above their heads. The shades of the room's two windows were partially drawn to darken the room just a bit. All three of them stared at the mysterious stranger who lay on his back in the bed beneath the patchwork quilt. His head was bandaged and the scratches on his face had been wiped clean.

Bob's thick, hairy arms were folded in front of him and rested on his belly. "So, you've never seen this man before in your life?" he asked.

"Never," Claire answered.

"Should we call the police?" Mildred chimed in.

"He asked me not too."

Cam entered the room. "Well, I walked a couple blocks in each direction and it didn't look like anyone was out lookin' fer this gentleman. Didn't see any signs of an abandoned vehicle, or an accident, or anything unusual."

"Hmm," Bob grunted.

"Someone must be missin' him. He came from somewhere" Mildred stated matter-of-factly. "Good-lookin' young man like this don't just drop outta the sky." She poked Claire in the ribs. "Us ladies just ain't that lucky."

Claire tried to hide her grin. Bob and Cam exchanged a glance and shook their heads.

"Come on, Mildred, let's walk downtown and grab a bite to eat for lunch," Cam suggested, turning and walking out of the room.

"We can't just leave Claire here with this man, What if he's a murderer, or rapist, or something … or … or worse." But it was too late; Cam was already out of earshot.

Bob lowered his brow and narrowed his eyes at Mildred. "What could be worse?"

"I don't know, but I'm sure there's worse."

"You go on, Mildred. I don't have to be anywhere till three. Besides, I don't think this guy is going to be too dangerous for the rest of the day," Bob said.

Mildred turned toward the door and patted Bob on the back as she walked by. "Okay, Bob. Would you like us to bring you back anything from the diner__, a sandwich or something?"

"No, Mildred, but thanks."

"How about you Claire__, anything?"

"No thanks, Mildred," Claire replied.

Bob stood next to Claire staring at the stranger's face. "What if he doesn't wake up?"

"What do you mean?"

"That lump on his head was pretty bad. I've always heard that you're not supposed to let someone fall asleep after a head injury. What if he just never wakes up?"

"If he's not awake by around noon tomorrow we'll have to call the police."

"You don't think we should just go ahead and call now?"

"The look in his eyes, Bob, when he asked me not to call the police, it was like he was begging."

"Maybe Mildred is right; maybe he's wanted by the law for something. He must be in some kind of trouble or he wouldn't have asked you not to call the police."

"If he wakes up tomorrow then he can tell us that. For now I'm going to give him the benefit of the doubt."

"Innocent until proven guilty, huh?"

"It's just a feeling I have, Bob."

Bob turned and walked to the door with a grin. "Women's intuition. Okay, okay I got it," he said, scratching the back of his head as he rounded the corner into the hall wondering what could have possibly happened.

Chapter Seven

Claire finished scooping the last of the raked leaves into a large black, plastic bag and dragged it to the other three bags she had placed near the front porch. Walking back to the middle of the yard to grab the rake, she scanned the property admiring her work. Before picking up the rake she looked at the dirt on her hands and wiped them on her jeans.

As she headed around the side of the house, rake in hand, she glanced up at the window of the room where she knew the stranger lay sleeping. *Who is he?* she wondered. *Where did he come from?* Mildred was right__, he was handsome. Claire thought about the way she felt as he lay on the lawn, helpless, his head in her lap, looking up into her eyes. At that moment she felt like a woman, she felt wanted… needed. She hadn't experienced those feelings in a long time and guilt nipped at her for having them now.

Claire continued across the patio and down the slate pathway that led to the garage at the rear of the house. Upon reaching the garage door, she grabbed a hold of the handle and with all her might lifted the aged wooden door. The springs and cables creaked as she pushed it up over her head to its upright position. When she let go, the door slowly began closing. Claire dropped the rake and grabbed the door with both hands and gave it a shove. This time it stayed put. Bending over to pick up the rake she sighed and whispered, "Stupid door."

*****

"I'm making myself a turkey sandwich, Bob," Claire called out from the kitchen. "Would you like one?"

Bob's ears perked up like a dog who had just heard the word *treat*. His chin lifted and he slowly rested the book he was reading in his lap. "What?" he hollered back. He knew what Claire had asked, but this was unusual. Had he heard her correctly?

Claire walked down the hallway and peeked into the parlor. "I asked if you would like a turkey sandwich."

"Um ... yeah, that would be great, thanks."

Claire's head disappeared from the doorway and she made her way back down the hall to the kitchen.

"You know," Bob called out after her, "you're going to have to change the sign out front to, bed and breakfast and lunch."

"Funny, Bob," Claire retorted over her shoulder. "I just thought I should at least feed you if you were going to stand guard over the stranger."

Bob grinned, lifted his book, and searched the page for where he had left off.

A few moments later Claire yelled from the dining room, "It's on the table, Bob. What would you like to drink?"

"Have you got a beer?"

"No."

"Milk?"

"Yeah."

"I'll have milk," Bob said, picking up from the end table the playing card he had been using as a bookmark, and he placed it in the book before closing it. He laid the book on the table and hoisted his large frame out of the chair with a groan.

As Bob got to the table and pulled out his chair, Claire was rounding the corner with his glass of milk. She placed the glass next to the plate that held his sandwich, chips, and pickle. Next to the plate was a fork and knife lying on top of a white paper napkin adorned with blue butterflies.

Bob plopped down in the chair. "Now that's service."

"Don't get used to it," Claire joked.

"Too late," Bob chuckled. He picked up the sandwich and bit off a mouthful. "Mmm, you sure open a mean package of lunch meat."

Claire gave Bob a playful slap on the shoulder and went back to the kitchen to get her own sandwich. When she returned, she sat at the end of the table. She took a sip of her milk and looked over at her guest and realized that she knew almost nothing about him. All of these years and they had never talked about anything but the weather and grab bars. Bob returned the look and gave her an uncomfortable grin.

"Are you married, Bob?" Claire asked.

Bob raised his eyebrows. "What?" The question seemed to catch him off guard.

"Married," Claire repeated. "Do you have a family?"

"I … uh," Bob squirmed uncomfortably in his chair, his chewing slowed, and he set his sandwich back on the plate. "I *was* married, Claire, a long time ago. My wife was … um, my wife—"

Suddenly a loud crash came from upstairs. Bob jumped instantly to his feet, his chair sliding across the hardwood floor and into the patio door behind him. Claire hadn't noticed him pick it up, but he was holding the knife she had laid next to his sandwich while he moved quickly down the hall toward the stairs.

Claire was amazed at how swiftly Bob had reacted. She was still standing at the head of the table as Bob stealthily made his way up the stairs. Realizing she still clung to her glass of milk, set it down and ran to join Bob.

When Claire reached the end of the hall, she looked up the stairs, but Bob was nowhere in sight. She trotted up the steps, and when she got to the top, she could see Bob through the doorway of room number four helping the stranger back to his bed.

"What happened?" Claire asked as she entered the room.

"Looks like your guest was going for a little stroll," Bob answered. "Probably smelled the turkey sandwiches."

Claire smirked. "Yeah, probably."

Bob got the stranger back into bed and covered him up with the blue and white quilt, then lingered at the edge of the bed.

The stranger opened his eyes. "Where am I?" he whispered. His voice was hoarse.

Claire spoke first. "I'm Cla—" Bob quickly raised his hand to shush her.

"You're in Dunquin Cove, Maine," Bob offered.

The stranger looked confused and his eyes scanned the bedroom.

"Where did you come from?" Claire asked.

The stranger shook his head no.

"Get him a glass of water, Claire."

The man warily looked around the room and then at Bob. "How long have I been here?"

"Four or five hours," Bob answered.

Claire returned from the bathroom with the small glass of water and handed it to Bob, who in turn offered it to the stranger.

"I was in a field," he said, then took a sip of the water. Little streams of water ran from the corners of his mouth and down his neck. A droplet hung from the cracked flesh of his bottom lip.

"Drink it slow," Bob instructed.

Claire looked down at the knife that was sticking out of Bob's back pocket. She wondered what his plan had been.

"What day is it?"

Bob ignored the question. "What's your name, pal?"

The stranger looked from Bob to Claire and then back to Bob. "I … I don't know.

Chapter Eight

"Amnesia?" Mildred asked, her eyebrows furrowed.

Claire nodded her head yes as she stared into the sauce pan of tomato soup she was stirring with a long wooden spoon.

"I never actually thought that was a real thing. I thought that it was just something made up for soap operas and movies," Mildred continued.

Cam stuck his head into the kitchen. "He's probably faking."

"Oh, Cam, you always think everyone is up to something," Mildred argued.

"Well, come on__, amnesia? What are the odds?"

"One hundred percent, if he's really got it," Mildred joked.

Claire grinned as she poured the soup into a bowl, which she had placed on the counter next to the stove. She placed the bowl on a silver tray alongside a turkey sandwich she had made, and then poured a glass of milk. She finished the arrangement with the milk, a napkin, and a spoon and knife on the tray.

"Let's not give him any weapons," Cam said pointing at the knife.

Claire picked up the knife, cut the sandwich in half, and placed the knife in the sink. After picking up the tray, she treaded cautiously toward the hall.

"Now that's service," Cam said. "Maybe I should go outside and smash my head on a rock or something."

"Cam," Mildred scolded.

Cam threw up his arms in defeat. "Sorry, sorry. But I am gonna head up there after he eats and have a talk with that young man. See if I can trip him up. See if he's really got this amnesia." Cam turned and followed Claire down the hall, turning when he got to the parlor while Claire went on up the stairs.

Claire pushed open the door with her foot and went in. The stranger lay on his back, his arms folded across his chest.

"I made you some soup and a sandwich, if you feel up to eating," Claire said, raising the tray slightly. "Do you like tomato soup?"

The stranger grinned. "I have no idea." He pushed himself up into a sitting position.

Claire grinned at his remark as she set the tray on his lap. "Be careful. It's hot." She turned and made her way across the room to the windows.

The stranger watched her as she walked away, his eyes passing over her shoulders, to her arms, then to her bottom. He watched as she bent over.

With her fingers she grabbed the bottom of the shade and gave it a tug, letting it slowly rise halfway up the window. She could feel his eyes upon her, and she tossed a looked over her shoulder. He quickly squinted from the sun and looked away.

"Is the light too much?" she asked.

"No, that's good."

Claire motioned toward the other window. "I'll leave the other one shut."

He picked up the glass of milk, sipped it and placed the glass on the nightstand. He took the spoon and dipped it into the soup, blowing on it as he brought it up to his mouth. "Mmm, that's good."

"It's an old recipe," Claire responded. "One can of soup to one can of milk."

He grinned and swallowed another spoonful. "The big guy, I heard him call you Claire."

"Bob."

He smiled. "Your name is Bob?"

Claire blushed. "No, *his* name is Bob. *My* name is Claire."

"That's good, because you don't look like a Bob."

"What should I call you?" Claire asked.

"Well, Claire and Bob are taken, so we can't use them. I'm fresh out of ideas."

"We can't keep calling you *that guy in room four*."

"If you had to guess my name, what would you guess?" He picked up the sandwich and took a bite.

Claire lowered her eyebrows and stared at his face. "Oh, I don't know." She tapped her finger on her chin as though she was in deep thought. "Maybe Ben, or maybe Rick. Something manly like that. Something rugged."

"So you think I'm rugged and manly?" he chuckled. "Nice."

Claire felt her face redden. "I just meant—"

"I know what you meant. I'm just joking with you. I think I'll go with Ben. That does sound ruggedly handsome."

"Okay, so Ben it is." Claire went to the door. "Put the tray on the nightstand when you're done." As she walked down the hall she called out, "It was rugged and manly, not rugged and handsome."

"Yeah, but I knew what you meant," Ben hollered back.

Chapter Nine

Claire was loading dishes into the dishwasher when she heard the front screen door slam. She glanced up at the clock on the wall above the sink, *3:25*. She knew it was Mica home from school. Then she heard the sound of the diesel engine rev as the school bus pulled away from the curb and made its way down the street.

She closed the dishwasher door and punched a couple buttons to start it. First there was a whirring and then the sound of rushing water. She started to walk away … until all of the sounds stopped at once. Claire turned and with a swift kick to the front of the dishwasher, the noises resumed. She shook her head as she went to the cookie jar to grab Mica's after-school snack.

"Mica," Claire called out as she set the plate of cookies and glass of milk on the table. Yet there was no answer.

She walked down the hall to the screen door, opened it and looked around the front yard. She noticed the three large bags of leaves were no longer sitting next to the front porch, they were now sitting on the lawn between the sidewalk and street. Claire turned, let the door close behind her, and perused the parlor. Cam sat on the couch watching the television that hung on the wall between the two front windows.

"Did you put the leaves out near the street?" she asked Cam.

"I did," he answered, never taking his eyes off the baseball game.

"You didn't have to do that."

"I know. I *wanted* to."

"How many times do I have to tell you, you're my guest here? You don't have to work."

Cam said. "I know, and right now I'm working on trying to hear the game."

Claire smiled. "Cam, have you seen Mica?"

"I have."

Claire waited for more to the story, but none came. "Where did you see him?"

Cam pointed his gnarled index finger straight up. "He came in and went upstairs."

Claire looked up the stairs and started up.

"Oh__, and Claire," Cam said, "we've decided not to leave tomorrow. Put us down for a couple more days."

Claire paused on the third step. "I thought you and Mildred wanted to be in Florida by Sunday."

"We did, but how could we leave now?"

"What do you mean?"

"Mysterious stranger, amnesia. Sounds like one of Mildred's soaps. This is the most excitement we've had on this whole trip. We've decided to hang around and see how it all plays out."

"Um … okay, Cam," Claire said tentatively as she started up the stairs. "I should charge extra for the show," she whispered to herself.

As Claire grabbed the wobbly wooden ball on the newel post at the top of the stairs, she could hear voices coming from room number four. She proceeded with soft steps and stopped just short of the door.

"How long are you staying?" she heard Mica ask.

"Not long," Ben answered.

"Where are you from?"

"Um … uh … nowhere in particular. I, uh, move around a lot."

"Where do you work?"

"I'm a bed and breakfast inspector."

"How do you like ours?"

"Well I haven't really ha—"

Claire leaned forward to get a better look, when suddenly the floor creaked beneath her. Both Mica and Ben looked toward the doorway.

"Mica," Claire said, walking into the room. "Let's let Mr. … let's let Ben rest. He's had a long trip."

"He's here to inspect our bed and breakfast, Mom," Mica explained.

"So I heard," Claire answered. "Mica, why don't you head on downstairs. There's cookies and milk on the table for you. You can start your homework when you're done."

Mica rose from where he sat at the edge of the bed. "Okay, Mom."

When Mica had left the room, Claire turned her attention back to Ben. "Bed and breakfast inspector?"

"It's the first thing that came to my mind."

Claire turned toward the door. "I hope we pass your inspection."

"So far, so good, Claire, but I will need to try some of those cookies."

*****

As Claire walked from the kitchen through the dining room, she grabbed the oversized cardigan that was hanging on the doorknob of the basement door and swung it, in one swift motion, around her back and up over her shoulders. She walked by the parlor and looked in to see Mica on his knees next to the coffee table. His English book was open and next to it lay a white sheet of paper. On the paper were sentences numbered from one through ten.

"Ya see, Mica," said Cam, who sat on the sofa peering over Mica's shoulder, "an adverb describes the verb. You know what a verb is?"

Mica nodded his head. "Yeah, like run, jump, sit. Stuff like that."

"That's right, the stuff yer doin'. Well, an adverb tells people how yer doin' it. For example, say yer runnin' down the road. How are ya runnin'? Are ya runnin' fast, or are ya runnin' slow?"

"I would probably be running fast," Mica said.

"That's right, so fast is the adverb. Ya get it?"

"I think so." Mica pointed at the first sentence and read, "The teacher spoke loudly in class today." He looked up at Cam. "Loudly is the adverb."

Cam grinned and mussed the hair on the top of the boy's head. "That's right, champ."

Mica grinned widely and turned back to his paper to circle the correct word.

Apparently sensing an onlooker, Cam looked up to see Claire standing in the doorway. "The boy's a genius, Claire," he stated.

"*Yer* a great English teacher, Cam," Claire returned in her best Mid-western drawl. At the sound of Cam's laughter she turned and pushed open the screen door and went out onto the front porch, letting the door smack closed behind her.

The sun had set and Claire stared at the purple sky above the houses across the street. She inhaled a deep breath. The air had cooled but was still warm for this time of year. A movement above her caught her attention, drawing her sight up at the porch light on the ceiling. Moths flew wildly around the light, darting toward it and then away. A slight breeze blew and the chains of the porch swing creaked. Claire sat in the swing. Over the past couple of years she had sat alone in the swing many times, but she would never get used to *having* to sit alone.

She pushed back with the heels of her sneakers and let the chair swing forward. *A glass of wine would be perfect right now*, she thought.

A man and a woman in their sixties walked by, their white Scottish terrier leading the way. The man looked over and waved. Claire smiled and waved back.

"Nice night," the man called out.

"Sure is," Claire hollered back.

The small dog barked and stopped for a moment to smell the fire hydrant. The couple stopped as well. When the dog had gotten all of the information it needed, he moved on.

"Won't be many more of these nights this year," the man's wife commented.

Claire watched the pair walk hand-in-hand until they were out of view. She continued looking up the street at a set of headlights that were coming her way. As the car neared, she recognized the big black Cadillac as it took a wide turn into the driveway and came to an abrupt halt. The door swung open and out climbed Bob Phillips. He slammed the door behind him and opened the backseat door. Leaning inside the car, he pulled out a briefcase, pushed a button on his keychain that popped open the trunk, and placed the briefcase in the trunk. Bob put both hands on the trunk lid and closed it. Dropping his car keys into the pocket of his sport coat, he suspiciously looked up the street one way and then the other direction.

As Bob shuffled up the walkway, he noticed Claire in the swing.

"Oh, hey, Claire," Bob said. "I didn't see you sitting there. Beautiful night, isn't it?"

"That's the consensus, Bob. How was your afternoon?"

Bob looked down at his muddy shoes and the cuffs of his pants. "Well if every hotel and motel in the area would pave their parking lots and walkways I would have had a better day. I swear, if I had a dollar for every puddle I stepped in today, I could retire."

Claire smiled. "Maybe you should start selling asphalt too."

"Maybe," Bob said as he kicked off his shoes, picked them up, and went through the door.

Claire folded her arms in front of her and watched two squirrels play in the yard across the street before scampering up into a tree to settle down for the night.

Chapter Ten

"Can I go up and say hi?" Mica asked.

"No," Claire answered. "You can talk to him when you get home from school. Now get your backpack on, the school bus will be here any minute."

"Do you think he is staying for the weekend?"

"I don't know, Mica. Keep moving." Claire could hear the school bus as it rounded the corner and made its way down their street.

"Do you think he will be here for the Harvest Festival?"

Claire nudged her son down the hallway toward the front door. "I don't know; that's almost a week away. I'm sure he will be gone by then." She opened the door and Mica ran for the bus. Claire let out a quick sigh of relief as she pushed the door closed.

"Claire," came Bob's voice from behind her.

Claire stepped back from the door and peeked into the parlor. Bob stood in the middle of the room, a cup of coffee in one hand, his other hand tucked in his inside jacket pocket. He pulled out a business card. "Claire, here is my cell number. I don't really like the idea of leaving you alone here with this guy. Had I known that Cam and Mildred were going to be down in York Harbor all day, I would have canceled my appointments for today."

Claire took the card and read it. "Thanks, Bob, but I'm sure everything will be fine."

"That's just in case you need me. This guy does anything you think is just a little strange, you give me a call and I'll be right back here. You understand? Anything."

Claire slipped the card into the side pocket of her cardigan. "Thanks, Bob, you're a good friend. I'm really glad you're here this week."

Bob beamed and patted Claire on the shoulder as he walked by. He stopped in front of the mirror, adjusted his tie, and disappeared out the door.

When the door closed, Claire looked up the stairs and thought about her guest. *Is he awake yet? Is he hungry? Would he like some breakfast?* She wondered. She put her hand on top of the newel post, went up two steps, and paused. She had gone to sleep thinking about him, she thought about him when she awoke this morning, and now she couldn't wait to see him. It was completely unlike her.

Claire turned and started back down the steps as she tried to shake off her feelings. She stopped again, unable to resist the temptation to look back up the stairs. *What am I doing?* she thought. As if her teenage schoolgirl-self whispered in her ear, she smirked, twisted and went up.

Claire knocked lightly on the door of room number four. She listened—silence. So she reached down and grabbed the door knob, slowly turning it to avoid alerting her guest of her presence. The knob clicked and she pushed open the door a few inches.

"Ben?"

There was still no answer so she peeked around the door, but the bed was empty and the covers were pulled back. Claire walked in.

Claire heard the click of the bathroom door just as it swung open. Her eyes darted to Ben's naked chest as he emerged from the bathroom. The hair on Ben's chest was wet and lay flat against his toned brown flesh. With a mind of their own, her eyes traveled down to the towel that was wrapped around his waist and then to his face.

Claire felt her face flush. "I … uh … I … um, the door," she stuttered, pointing back at the door. "It was unlocked. I'm sorry; I didn't know you were naked … I mean—"

Ben put his hand up, gesturing her to stop. "It's okay. I should have locked the door."

Claire stepped back toward the door. "I was just coming up to see if you were awake and if you wanted something for breakfast."

"Yes, that would be great, Claire. Um, what did you do with my clothes?" Ben asked, scanning the bedroom.

"I washed them; they're down in the laundry room, but the pants and shirt were pretty ripped up. I think I might have something for you to wear in my room. I'll be right back." Claire gripped the doorknob and then turned back to Ben. "There is a new toothbrush in that top drawer in the vanity."

"Thank you." Ben watched as she left the room.

Claire traipsed down the hall and made the turn into her bedroom. Walking past the full-length mirror as she meandered to her closet, she paused and ran her fingers through her hair. She looked at the baggy, gray shirt she was wearing, then at the faded jeans that she had rolled up twice at the bottom of each leg, and lastly at her bare feet.

She turned toward the closet doors and stared at them for a long second before opening them. Then she reached her hand into the closet and slid articles of clothing down the closet rod one at a time until she came to what she was looking for. Grabbing a hanger she pulled out a pair of men's jeans and tossed them onto her bed. She stuck her hand back into the clothing and yanked out a faded red flannel shirt and lay it on top of the jeans.

Claire then walked to her dresser and, opening the bottom drawer, pulled out a pair of men's flannel boxers, a white t-shirt, and a grey pair of socks. She closed the drawer and walked back to her bed. Picking up the jeans and shirt, she pressed them to her face and took a deep breath, smelling the shirt that her husband had once wore. Three years' time had faded his scent and the shirt just smelled like a shirt, but Claire could still remember what he smelled like. Some nights, still, she would wake up in the middle of the night and swear she could smell his presence. On particularly nostalgic evenings she would even put on one of his shirts and wear it to bed. And now another man would be wearing his clothes...

Claire wasn't sure how to feel about that.

Chapter Eleven

Ben sat in a chair at the dining room table, his back to the patio door. He looked across the table through a doorway and into another room that seemed to be set up as a makeshift office. There was a green and red plaid couch on the far wall facing him, and behind it two large windows. On the wall to his left were a computer and printer on a small desk. On the wall to the right was a closed door.

Dishes clanked together in the kitchen and Ben could hear Claire's bare feet moving across the ceramic tile floor. He looked up at the antique chandelier that hung above the table and then at the fancy decorative crown molding.

"I have milk or coffee, and there's a little bit of orange juice left," Claire called out from the kitchen.

Ben looked to the kitchen doorway. "Coffee would be great, thanks."

Claire came into the dining room with the coffee sloshing around in a large white cup and she sat it in front of him. "It's from this morning. If it's too strong, I can make another pot."

"I'm sure it's fine," Ben said. He turned the cup to get a better look at the big red lobster on the side of it. Next to the lobster, in red letters it said; *Dunquin Cove Maine.* He blew on the hot coffee and took a sip as Claire returned to the kitchen.

"How is your head this morning?" Claire asked.

"My headache is gone but this lump on the back of my head hurts when I push on it," Ben answered, rubbing the back of his head.

Claire walked back into the room and set a plate before him with two eggs over-medium, three strips of bacon, and two slices of buttered toast. She smiled. "Then don't push on it," she said.

"Good advice."

Claire was almost back into the kitchen when Ben asked, "Did you already eat?"

"Yes."

"Can you sit with me while I eat? I have a few questions."

Claire turned. "Sure." She sat down adjacent to Ben at the head of the table.

Ben cut his eggs into tiny pieces as Claire watched. "I could have scrambled those for you," she said.

Ben looked up from his mangled eggs. "What? Oh, I've always cut up my e—" He paused. "How did I know that that's how I cut up my eggs?"

Claire stared into his eyes and shrugged her shoulders. "I'm sure eventually everything will come back to you."

Ben scooped up some of the eggs with his fork and put them in his mouth. "It's weird," he said. "I know how to walk and talk. Christ, I even know how I like my eggs, but I don't know my name or where I came from."

Claire placed her hand on top of Ben's. She tried to think of some words that might comfort him, but she feared that the words would come out sounding like some cheap romance novel. As quickly as she touched him, she took her hand away.

Ben bit into the piece of toast and then gulped a swig of coffee. "Claire, was there anything in my pants pocket, a wallet … anything?"

"Nothing. There was a five and two ones in your shirt pocket."

An image flashed in Ben's mind. It was of a gas station. A hand reached through the rear window of a car. *Here's your change, pal*, someone said. *Who was that*? he thought. *Who said that*? Ben rubbed his eyes with the tips of his finger and thumb.

"Did you remember something?" Claire asked.

"No … no, it was nothing."

"It'll come, give it time."

"Do you have a map?"

"Sure, there's a map of the whole area on the wall over the desk," Claire said, pointing into the next room.

There was a thud out on the front porch and Claire stood up from the table.

"Who's here?" Ben asked.

"No one. That was the newspaper." She got up from her seat and started down the hall toward the front door. "The kid who used to deliver it quite a few weeks ago, so now there's no telling what time it will get here."

Ben relaxed in his chair and sipped his coffee. Looking into the office, he thought about the map on the wall and got up to take a look. The map was right where Claire had said it was; Ben leaned in for a closer look. Putting his index finger on the dot marked Dunquin Cove, he followed Shore Road south to York Harbor and then north to Ogunquit. He stepped back and rubbed his temples.

Claire tossed the paper on the dining room table and joined him in the office. "Everything okay?" she asked.

"My headache is coming back. You wouldn't have a few aspirins, would you?"

"Coming right up," Claire responded. She grabbed Ben's breakfast dish as she walked by the table and into the kitchen.

Ben tilted his head toward the doorway. "Claire?"

"Yes?" she hollered back from the kitchen.

"What way was I coming from?"

Claire returned to the office with a glass of water. She held out her hand and opened her palm, holding four aspirins. "Which direction?" she repeated the question. "You were coming from the south."

Ben looked back at the map. "The only place I could have come from is York."

"Unless you got off the interstate."

"But then where is my car?" Ben took the aspirins and threw them to the back of his throat, took the glass of water and washed them down. "Thanks, Claire. And if I was with someone else, why would they just drive away and leave me in some field on the side of the road?"

"A field?" Claire inquired.

"Yes. When I woke up I was lying in a big field just outside of town. I remember walking to the road and seeing a road sign. I couldn't remember what the sign said or which direction I was walking. It's all a little fuzzy still." He rubbed the lump on his head and winced in pain.

Claire took the glass back from Ben. "Why don't you go sit down and rest?"

"Good idea. If I stand for too long I start feeling dizzy … and my ribs are killing me." Ben lifted the side of his shirt to inspect the bruises on his ribs.

Claire admired his well-developed abs and then quickly looked away and went to the kitchen. "You go sit down, I have to get this kitchen cleaned up."

Chapter Twelve

Ben awoke on the sofa in the parlor, cautiously peering around the room. It took him a few seconds to remember where he was. His head was resting on the arm of the sofa, and a small patchwork quilt had been thrown over his torso while he slept. He looked at the clock on the wall, over the fireplace. *12:30*. He lay quietly listening for sounds that might tell him who was now home and where in the house Claire might be. In the almost total silence of the empty house the hum of the refrigerator's motor was all he could hear.

He sat up and soon realized that his headache had been replaced by a stiff neck, thanks to the hard arm of the sofa. Ben inched toward the edge of the couch, tilted his head one way and then the other. *Crack!* At that moment his neck released the pressure.

Ben folded the quilt and threw it over the back of the couch and went to explore. He walked out of the living room and shot a look up the stairs as he went down the hall toward the dining room.

"Claire," he called out, but quietly. There was no answer.

He peeked his head through the kitchen doorway. The kitchen was long and narrow with dark wood cupboards, Formica counter tops that were the color of granite, and a light brown ceramic tile floor. At the other end of the kitchen was a doorway with steps leading downward to the basement, and to the right a door that led back into the office.

Ben turned and walked back into the dining room, heading for the patio door. Opening it he walked down a set of wooden steps that led to a slate patio. The slate had been laid long ago on top of the grass and had now sunken into the earth to ground level. Grass sprouted up between each piece of slate. Ben took his bare foot and with the tip of his toe scraped at the thin layer of moss that grew on the surface of the slate.

In the middle of the patio was a green table with a glass top and four matching chairs. Just beyond the patio was a line of cedar trees that ran the full length of the property, cutting off any view of the house next door.

Ben ambled around the property and then found his way to the back of the house. A blacktop driveway that ran down the other side of the house turned across the back yard separating the yard from the garage. To the right of the garage was more yard with two large maple trees.

A pile of leaves sat next to the driveway, and next to it was a rake. Ben looked around for Claire and then went to see if she was in the garage. "Claire," he called out once again, as he entered the garage.

The garage was dark, and he fumbled around for a light switch. Finding one, he flipped it on but nothing happened. He looked up at the single fixture bulb dangling from the ceiling and flipped the switch off and on again with the same outcome. A minivan was parked in the garage, so he rounded it on his way to the back of the building. At the rear of the garage was a tool bench, and hanging above it on the wall were several hand tools. Lying on the bench was a circular saw, a jig saw, and a few other power tools. He picked up a couple of the tools, examined them, and then placed them back on the bench.

A photograph was stuck to the wall with a tiny nail. Ben pulled out the nail with one fingernail and grabbed the picture with the other to get a closer look in the dark. Claire was in the picture, as well as Mica and standing next to them was a man. The man and Mica were wearing matching baseball caps, although Mica wore a Little League uniform. They stood behind home plate with the backstop at their backs, all three were grinned broadly. He wondered where the man was now. *Happier days*, he thought.

Ben pushed the nail back through the picture into the same hole he had removed it from, then walked down the other side of the minivan. He paused at the window and looked out, seeing through the trees into the neighbor's yard. *Great*, he thought, *they've got a hot tub on their patio. I should have stumbled into their yard.* He pressed his fingertips against his aching ribs and walked out into the driveway. The sun was bright and he rubbed his eyes with the palms of his hands until his pupils adjusted.

"Can I help you?" came a deep voice from Ben's left, startling him. He turned to see a man dressed in dark blue pants, matching button-up short sleeved shirt, and a shiny badge on his chest. The man's torso was puffed out like a peacock looking for love, and his hands rested on his gun belt. His light brown hair was cut short and his eyes were hidden behind a pair of gold-rimmed aviators. He was about the same build and height as Ben. The officer had one large pimple on his forehead and another to the left of his cleft chin.

"I ... uh," Ben stammered, pointing back at the garage.

"You a guest here?"

"No ... I mean yes, well kind of."

"Either you are or you aren't, fella," the officer said, moving his hand over slightly and resting it on the grip of his pistol.

"Well I'm sta—"

"Where's your shoes?"

Ben looked down at his bare feet and wiggled his toes.

"You have some ID on ya, fella?"

Ben's instinct told him to run, but where too was the question. He looked down at his bare feet again and then back at the officer. Ben opened his palms in a show of surrender. "I'm just gonna go back inside," he said, moving slowly toward the patio door. "My shoes and identification are in the house."

"Hold on, hold on, pal. I didn't say you could go anywhere." The officer wrapped his fingers around the handle of his pistol.

Ben's eyes darted to the gun.

"Chet, what's going on?" The screen door at the rear of the house creaked open. It was Claire, with a laundry basket resting on her hip.

The officer released his grip on his weapon and Ben could see his shoulders relax a little.

"Chet, I asked you what was going on," she repeated. "What are you doing back here?" Claire pushed the door the rest of the way open and walked outside. Setting the basket on the grass, she started toward Ben.

Officer Chet nodded toward Ben. "I caught this guy going through your garage. I noticed that he wasn't wearing any shoes and he seemed like he was up to something."

Claire walked up to Ben's side and put her arm around him. "*This guy*," she informed, "is Clay's brother."

Ben gave a crooked grin. *Who's Clay?* he wondered.

"Clay's brother?" Chet asked, lowering his brow.

Ben stuck out his hand and walked over to Chet. "Yeah, I'm Ben, Clay's brother, fella."

Chet took his hand and gave it a shake. "I didn't remember Clay saying he had a brother." Chet stared into Ben's eyes as he spoke.

"That's okay," Ben said with a relieved smile. "Half the time I can't remember what happened yesterday."

Claire shot him a look and shook her head.

"It's a pleasure to meet you, Ben. Name's Chet, I'm part of the police force here in Dunquin Cove. I like to check in on Mrs. Dunning and Mica from time to time, being here alone and all, and with strangers coming and going all the time."

"Well that's very nice of you, officer …" Ben looked at the brass name tag on Chet's shirt.

"Mr. Dunning, you can just call me Chet."

"Well then you can just call me Ben."

"Okay then." Chet stared at Claire for a few seconds, looked around the property and then started slowly walking backward down the driveway. "I'll see you later, Mrs. Dunning. I'll drive by again later."

"Thanks, Chet," Claire said and gave a little wave.

Chet strode confidently to the corner of the house and when he was out of sight Ben could hear his shoes slap the blacktop as he headed to his patrol car.

"Someone's got a crush on Mrs. Dunning," Ben sang.

Claire picked up her laundry basket and pulled open the back door. "Oh please," she responded. "He's only in his early twenties."

Ben followed her through the door. "Really? I thought he was about fourteen."

Chapter Thirteen

Ben sat on the couch and tied the white canvas Converse sneakers Claire had provided for him. When he finished tying them he pressed his thumb into the toe of the shoe. *A little big*, he thought. He wiggled his toes and marched in place a few steps trying out his new shoes. *Good enough.*

Ben walked down the hallway toward the dining room, the sneakers squeaking on the hardwood floor with every step. He paused at the dining room table and rubbed the bottoms of the shoes on the rug underneath the table, hoping to wear off the squeak. Yet when he began walking again, the squeaking continued. He rolled his eyes and headed into the kitchen.

When he poked his head through the kitchen door, the dishwasher hummed and a small radio on the countertop next to the sink played "Tequila Sunrise." Ben listened for a moment and realized that he knew every word. He smiled, shook his head, and walked to the door at the other end of the kitchen.

When he got to the door, the music stopped and Ben paused.

That was the Eagles with "Tequila Sunrise." It's one o'clock and you're listening to Dunquin Cove's own 104.2. How about this weather, folks? Sunny and seventy-six. Let's hope it sticks around for the harvest festival. Here's Howard with the local news. What's going on today Howard?

Ben stepped back toward the radio.

Well, Larry, tonight's town meeting is at seven and all are welcome to attend. The main topics are expected to be whether or not to remove the flashing red light from the corner of Main and Elizabeth, and should we or should we not raise the price on parking meters between May and September. Also, the identities of the two men killed in a single-car accident out on Shore Road in the early morning hours yesterday have still not been identified. A statement released by the state police says that the car they were driving had been stolen in upstate New York a few days before the accident.

Ben listened for anyone around before shutting off the radio. Had it been coincidence, or was he involved somehow?

He jogged to the dining room table, grabbed the newspaper Claire had tossed there earlier in the day, and unfolded it. At the top of the front page it read; AUTHORITIES SEEKING IDENTIFICATION OF CRASH VICTIMS.

Ben refolded the newspaper and went back into the kitchen; he scanned the room for a garbage can but didn't see one. He reached up and tossed the paper on top of one of the wall cabinets, out of sight, and headed outside through the kitchen door.

Through the door a set of stairs led to a landing at ground level where a door exited into the backyard. On the side of the landing another set of steps turned and went to the basement. He walked down to the landing and looked down the stairs into the darkness of the basement and could hear the washing machine and dryer running. Resisting the urge to snoop, he went out the back door.

Claire was in the backyard, once again working on the leaves.

"How about if I do that," Ben offered.

"That's okay, I got it," Claire replied.

"I know," he said, taking the rake. "But it's the least I can do. After all, you loaned me these great shoes and all."

She smiled. "Thank you. I'm just used to doing everything around here myself."

Ben began raking the leaves into the pile that Claire had already started. "What do you do with the leaves once they're in a pile?"

Claire pointed toward the garage. "There's some black plastic bags on the bench at the back of the garage. I fill them up and then drag them out to the curb."

"Was Clay your husband?" Ben asked.

The question caught Claire off guard. Her voice cracked. "Yes."

"That him in the pictures on the garage wall?"

"Yes."

Ben continued to rake. "Where is he now?"

"He passed away three years ago__, cancer."

"Sorry."

Ben dropped the rake on the lawn and disappeared into the garage. When he returned he was holding two plastic bags, one of which he dropped on the grass and the other he handed to Claire. "You want to hold this open for me? I'll fill it up."

Claire shook the large bag a few times, filling it with air, and held it open for Ben.

"How do the shoes fit?" she asked.

"Perfect," Ben lied, for some strange reason not wanting Claire to know that her husband's feet were larger than his own.

"Headache?"

"I feel a lot better. The ribs are still pretty sore." Ben removed his flannel shirt, tossed it on the ground, and then lifting the bottom of his T-shirt he wiped the sweat from his brow.

"I bet. That's some bruise."

Ben scooped up a large handful of leaves and dropped them in the bag. "How long have you had this place?"

"About seven years. Clay was a teacher at York Community College for twelve years and I worked over at the hospital in Portsmouth. We saved up and bought this place. I quit my job first to run the bed and breakfast and then a year later Clay resigned to help me."

"Were you a nurse?"

"No. I worked in an office ... billing."

When the bag was full, Ben slid it over in front of him and tied the bag closed. He picked up the rake and moved to another part of the yard and began raking. "What's the story with officer Chet?"

"What do you mean?"

"Well most cops don't ride by and check on someone's house a few times a day."

Claire laughed. "He was a student of Clay's. When he was younger he would help out a little around here and Clay would pay him. When Clay passed away Chet took it pretty hard. I guess he just feels like it's part of his job to protect us now."

When all the leaves were raked up, Claire reached down and picked up the other bag and opened it. Ben threw the leaves in the bag handfuls at a time until the pile was gone. He picked up the bag without tying it, then hoisted the other bag over his shoulder.

Claire watched his biceps flex as he lifted the bags. "You can just put them by the back door and I'll bring them around front later."

"Will do," Ben answered.

"I better get back to the laundry."

Ben opened the door and held it for Claire as she walked in, took a right, flipped on the light switch, and went down the cellar stairs. After she disappeared around the corner, Ben went up the stairs and into the kitchen. Placing his hand atop the cabinet, he felt for the paper, found it, and pulled it down. He went back down the stairs and, glancing down into the basement to make sure Claire couldn't see him, he opened the back door and shoved the newspaper down into the open bag. Grabbing one side of the bag in each hand, he tied the bag closed.

Chapter Fourteen

Ben sat on the steps of the bed and breakfast with a small paintbrush in his hand and a quart of flat black paint on the step next to him. He dipped the brush in the paint and spread it on the wrought iron; a bristle came loose from the brush and stuck to the railing. With his fingertips he carefully pulled the stray bristle away and wiped it on the rag that lay next to the can, and then smoothed out the mark that had been left in the paint.

Setting the brush down across the top of the paint can, Ben took the back of his hand and wiped the beads of sweat from his forehead and then wiped his hand on the leg of his pants. He lifted his arm and looked at the sweat stains in the armpit of his t-shirt, and then up at the bright sun staring down at him.

The screen door squeaked open and Claire stood holding a pitcher of lemonade and two glasses on a tray.

"I can't believe it's this hot," Ben said.

Claire pushed the door fully open with her hip and walked through it onto the porch. "Not your average fall day in Maine. I made some lemonade. Why don't you take a break?"

"Sounds good to me. Thanks."

Claire set the tray down on the glass top table nestled next to the door, picked up the pitcher, poured a glass full, and handed it to Ben. She then poured a glass of lemonade for herself and sat down. Ben thought about sitting next to her but sat back down on the top step.

"That's just what I needed," Ben said, taking a big gulp.

Claire sat contemplatively for a moment and then said, "I feel funny putting you to work like this."

Ben laughed. "Hey, it was my idea. It's a small price to pay for an all-inclusive vacation in Maine." Ben took another drink from his glass and felt the ice click against his teeth. He had a sudden craving for a cigar and furrowed his brow.

Claire noticed and asked, "What's the matter?"

"Nothing," Ben answered, shaking off the feeling. He took another gulp and placed the empty glass on the porch floor.

"Want some more?" Claire leaned toward the pitcher.

Ben picked up the glass. "Yes, please."

Both looked up as a familiar car went past them, took a left into the driveway, and drove to the back of the house. It was Cam and Mildred's 2013 black Buick Lacrosse. A few minutes later they appeared around the front of the house and walked down the stone path that led from the driveway to the porch steps. Mildred was holding a white plastic bag in one hand and a green plastic bag in the other. Cam was also holding the same types of bags, one in each hand.

Cam raised his bags in the air. "Guess who bought a bunch of useless crap in York Harbor?"

Mildred sneered. "We got some nice stuff; don't listen to this old fool."

"Nice stuff," Cam repeated. "She bought a little Nubble Lighthouse to put toothpicks in."

Claire laughed. "Sounds like a nice souvenir to me, Mildred."

"We both wear dentures," Cam responded.

Ben laughed out loud as he dipped the paintbrush into the can and resumed his chore.

"I see ya put this young man to work," Mildred said.

Claire raised her hands in defense. "It was his idea."

Cam put both bags in one hand and slapped Ben on the back as he walked by him and up the steps. "Good man, good man. If anyone needs me I'll be upstairs taking a nap." Cam opened the front door and went in. Mildred followed him up the steps.

"Be careful, ma'am. The railing is wet," Ben said.

As Mildred made her way past Ben, she made eye contact with Claire and nodded her head back toward Ben and winked with a sly grin. Claire shook her head and looked out over the street. Mildred giggled as she went into the house, catching Ben's attention as his eyes followed her inside before tossing a look at Claire with a puzzled expression on his face. Claire shrugged her shoulders as to say, *I don't know.*

Ben went back to painting the railing as Claire sipped her drink and gently swung back and forth in the swing.

Chapter Fifteen

Ben stood at the back of the garage, squinting to read the labels of the various jugs, jars, and containers that sat in the darkness on a decrepit wooden bookcase that had long ago been turned into a makeshift shelving unit. Instinctively he had flipped on the light switch when he walked through the garage door before remembering that the light didn't work.

He grabbed a quart can and read it; *linseed oil*. Ben didn't know what linseed oil was, but he knew it wasn't what he was looking for, so he set the can back down and resumed the search. A package of light bulbs caught his eye and he pulled them down off the shelf. Reaching up over his head he unscrewed the existing bulb and replaced it. He walked back to the garage door and turned on the switch__, the garage lit up.

Ben returned to the shelf and grabbed a plastic gallon jug of paint thinner, set it on the bench, and took down a coffee can that had been sitting next to the paint thinner. There were a few rusted screws and nails in the can, so he dumped them onto the bench and poured the paint thinner into the empty can. He placed the paint brush into the thinner, sloshed it back and forth a few times, and left it to soak.

When Ben exited the garage, he noticed the two bags of leaves sitting next to the back door, thought about the newspaper hiding within, and decided he better take them around front to the curb. He picked up a bag in each hand. As he walked down the driveway along the black iron fence that surrounded the front yard, he could see the school bus making its way down the street. Just as he set the bags on the curb, the bus came to a stop and the brakes let out a squeal before a hissing sound of the air brakes engaged. Ben stepped back onto the sidewalk as the bus driver swung a lever, opening the door. The bus driver nodded, and Ben nodded back. When Mica got to the top of the steps, the driver stuck out his arm halting the boy.

"You know this guy?" the driver asked.

Mica nodded his head yes. Ben stepped toward the bus and climbed up one step, sticking out his hand.

"Ben," he said. "Ben Dunning."

Mica looked puzzled but smiled.

The driver took Ben's hand and shook. "Oh sorry, Mr. Dunning, ya can't be too careful nowadays. A lot of bad guys out there."

"You got that right," Ben returned. "You got that right."

Mica slung his book bag over his shoulder and jumped down the steps to the sidewalk. Together they stood and watched as the door swung shut and the bus left for its next stop.

"You have the same last name as me?" Mica asked.

Ben laid his hand on top of Mica's head and mussed his hair. "You better ask your mother about that, kid."

"Okay." Mica handed his book bag to Ben. "Can you hold this for me? I have to tie my shoe."

Ben took the bag. "Sure."

Mica bolted for the front door. "Haha, gotcha."

Ben looked down at the bag in his hand and shook his head. "Good one," he called out.

Mica ran through the front door and down the hall, heading straight for the cookies and milk that had been left for him on the dining room table.

Claire exited the office when she heard the front door slam. "Where is your book bag?" she asked.

"Mr. *Dunning* wanted to carry it for me," Mica answered.

"Mr. Dunning?"

"Yeah, Mom, he told Mr. Watson that his name was Ben Dunning. Why did he tell him that?"

"He did?"

Ben walked into the room and plopped Mica's book bag down next to him.

"Yes," Mica answered.

Claire looked to Ben. "You told the bus driver that your name was Ben Dunning?"

"I was just following suit," Ben answered.

"Are you related to us?" Mica asked.

"Yes," Ben responded.

"No," Claire blurted out. "We just told a couple people that he was related to us."

"Why?"

Claire looked to Ben for help. "Because …"

"Because," Ben cut in, "I can't remember my real name. So we're just going to pretend that my name is Ben Dunning until I remember what my real name is."

Claire watched Mica's eyes for his reaction.

Before Mica could utter a word, Cam appeared in the door way.

"How did you forget your name?" Mica finally asked after a moment.

"You ever hear of amnesia?"

"Yeah, like when someone gets hit on the head and can't remember anything," Mica answered proudly.

"That's right," Claire said.

Mica looked back at Ben. "You hit your head?"

"Yeah."

"How?"

"Can't remember."

"Do you have kids?"

"Don't know."

"Maybe if you do they're worried about you."

"Maybe."

"Did you call the cops?"

"Can't call the cops."

"Why?"

"Can't remember."

"It's 911," Mica said.

"I remember the *number*, I just can't remember why I can't call them."

Mica's eyes lit up. "Maybe you're a spy and you were on a mission and something went wrong."

Claire intervened. "Okay, okay, that's enough questions. Eat your cookies and drink your milk."

As Mica shoveled a cookie into his mouth, he muttered, "Do you remember if you like cookies?"

"That's the one thing I'm pretty sure of__, I do love cookies," Ben answered with a smile.

"Ya hear that, Mom? He loves cookies."

"I heard," she said before wandering back into the kitchen.

Ben rested his hands on the table and leaned in close to Mica's ear. "We can't be positive that I'm not a spy, Mica, so we have to keep this whole thing a secret." Ben looked back at Cam and winked. "Can you keep a secret, Mica?"

"Yes."

"Good. So if anyone asks, I'm your Uncle Ben."

"Just like the guy on the box of rice," Cam added.

"I won't tell anyone," Mica said before tossing another cookie into his mouth.

Ben pushed away from the table and turned to Cam. "Just like the guy on the box of rice?"

Cam grinned slyly. "Hey, just be glad their last name is Dunning and not Dover."

Chapter Sixteen

"Where's our forgetful guest?" Bob asked as he walked up the front steps.

Claire sat in the chair swing, her hair pulled back into a ponytail. She was wearing jeans and a blue t-shirt with white print that read

104.2

BIG LARRY IN THE MORNING.

Over the t-shirt she was wearing a dark blue cardigan. Bob noticed that Claire was wearing a little more makeup than usual and her lips glistened with a pink gloss.

"He's doing the dishes," she responded with a slight grin.

"Making himself right at home."

"He's just trying to help out." Even as the words left her lips she wondered why she was explaining herself to another guest.

Bob rested a warming hand on Claire's shoulder. "Be careful, Claire."

As Claire held back her retort Bob went on into the house. The door had just slammed shut when it opened again and out came Ben.

"Nice night," he said.

"Yup," Claire answered.

Ben sat down on the top step and the door swung open again.

"Are ya sure you don't want to take the car?" Cam asked.

"It's a beautiful night for a walk," Mildred answered.

"It's two miles away."

"It's six blocks."

"I'm an old man." Cam let out a groan as he hobbled dramatically down the steps.

Mildred looked to Claire. "We're gonna walk over to that diner on Main Street and get a little something for dinner. Want us to bring you back anything?"

"No, thanks," Claire answered.

Mildred nudged Ben in the back with her knee. "How about you, young fella?"

"No thanks Mildred. I just ate."

"Okay then, we'll be back later." Mildred trotted down the steps and joined her husband at the front gate. Cam reached down and flipped up the latch and opened the gate for his wife, then followed her out and shut it behind him. Claire and Ben watched as the old couple made their way down the sidewalk. Just before they were out of sight Cam reached over and took his wife's hand. Ben peeked over and noticed the glow on Claire's face as she watched them with genuine delight.

"It is a nice night for a walk," Ben said.

"It is," Claire agreed.

"We could go for a walk and you could show me around your little town," Ben offered.

"Sure," Claire answered, a little faster than she had wanted to. "Let me run upstairs and tell Mica we'll be gone for a little while."

*****

The cool breeze was refreshing as it tousled Claire's hair. Walking comfortably close to Ben, the followed Shore Road for a few blocks until they came to Main Street. Claire paused at the corner. "Left is toward the business district; right will take us down by the cove."

"Let's walk down by the water," Ben decided.

Claire turned and waited on the curb until the traffic cleared and they both crossed. As they reached the other side of the street, Ben noticed a curvy woman sitting on a bench in front of a store. Her dark hair was graying with age and she wore it up in a tight bun. Ben guessed her age at sixty. She wore black stretch pants that were exceeding their limit, a large white t-shirt, and a full-length red apron with spots of chocolate and flour. The sign over her head on the store front read, Lita's Bakery.

The woman on the bench said, "Good evening, Claire. Beautiful night for a walk."

"You can say that again, Lita," Claire answered.

"Is this your brother-in-law?" Lita asked as she ran her eyes up and down Ben.

Claire looked puzzled. "Yes, how did you know th—?"

Lita threw a thumb over her shoulder at a willowy man working behind the counter in the bakery. "Howard told me. He said he was having lunch with Frank today at the diner and Frank told him that he ran into Chet, and Chet told *him*."

Claire rolled her eyes. "Word spreads fast."

Ben peered through the large window into the bakery and scanned the baked goods from shelf to shelf. Feeling her stare, Ben realized Lita hadn't taken her eyes off him. "See anything you like, handsome?" she suggested in a deep, sexy voice.

Ben's eyes widened. "I, uh … I was just looking at the cupcakes and stuff."

Lita cocked her head and stretched her neck to get a good look at Ben's behind. "Me too."

Ben gave a feigned fearful smile and looked to Claire for help.

The skinny beanpole of a man behind the counter was now leaning through the doorway. "Pick on someone your own age, Lita," he said.

Lita looked back toward the door. "I'll be picking on you tonight, Howard, now that this young man has gotten me in the mood." She glanced back at Claire and winked.

Howard sneered at Ben. "Thanks a lot, fella. What did I ever do to you?"

Ben threw up his hands. "Hey, I was just walking by."

Claire grabbed Ben by the arm. "We better get going; I told Mica we wouldn't be too long."

"You kids have a nice walk," Howard said as he turned to retreat inside. "And remember, pal, I owe ya one."

Lita let out a cackle as Ben and Claire continued on down the street. They had walked about half a block when Claire realized she was still holding Ben's forearm, then she let go. Ben looked down at his arm and then at Claire, who stared straight ahead so Ben decided not to comment.

The two walked on down the sidewalk past a candy store, a wine shop, and, on the corner of Main Street and Dunquin Lane, a small restaurant. Music could be heard from inside the restaurant, and Ben looked in through the large front windows. There were several round tables, more than half of which were occupied. At the far end of the room was a pool table, and beyond it a bar that ran the full length of the room, the bar was about half full. Ben wanted to go in and have a drink but he knew the seven or eight dollars Claire had found in his pocket was the only money he had, and probably wasn't enough. He looked up at the sign over the door. THE COVE.

As they stepped down off the curb and started across Dunquin Lane, Ben checked back to see a small deck attached to The Cove where guests could eat outdoors if they wanted. Two wooden swinging doors opened and a waitress backed through carrying large tray.

Claire crossed the street first, turned, and waited for Ben. "Hungry?" she asked.

"No. Looks like a nice place though." He stepped up on the curb.

"Very good seafood." Claire turned and walked to a railing that ran along the opposite side of the sidewalk. She rested her elbows on top of the rough-cut fence and stared out over the water. Ben followed suit in companionable silence.

Claire inhaled a deep breath of sea air. "I've lived here my whole life and I never tire of the smell of the ocean."

Ben was struck by the impressive jagged rocks below that met the sand, then further vanished into the lapping waves in the distance. He too took a deep breath. Claire looked over. "I couldn't resist," he said. She smiled.

The moon lit up the beach and they watched the people as they strolled along. Two couples held hands, a man walked his dog. Ben watched two seagulls hop along looking for scraps left behind by the day's beach goers and he thought of his bag of Doritos.

"Do you want to go down and walk on the beach?" Claire asked.

Ben looked around. "Sure."

"What are you looking for?"

"I was just wondering if there was a restroom close by that I could use."

"Um ... yes," Claire said, pointing across Main Street. "There's public restrooms over there between the insurance place and that ice cream shop, or you could use the bathroom in The Cove."

Ben started back toward the restaurant. "You want to wait here? I'll run in quick and use theirs."

Claire leaned her back against the fence. "I'll be here."

Ben stepped up on the deck, walked by the tables, pushed open the swinging doors, and went in. He nodded to the bartender as he went by and then saw a restroom sign over a short hallway. When he got to the men's room, he jiggled the handle. Locked.

As Ben waited he faced the wall looking at a bulletin board that was hanging over a small table. He folded his arms in front of himself and read the various ads. Piano lessons, fifteen dollars per class. Mini-bike for sale, two hundred dollars or best offer. Have you seen this man? Above the wording was the photograph of a man, probably in his mid-thirties, with light hair and a reddish goatee. There was a phone number and in the bottom left-hand corner it was dated three months earlier. Ben wondered if they ever found him, he wondered if there were posters somewhere else with *his* picture on them. Maybe in another state, another town, another restaurant.

A hand came down suddenly on Ben's shoulder. In one breathless fluid motion Ben raised his elbow, knocking the hand into the air, and then grabbed the man's wrist. He bent it upward and spun it behind the man's back, lifting upward. With his other hand Ben grabbed the hair on the back of the man's head and shoved his cheek against the wall.

"Whoa … whoa, buddy," the man gasped.

Ben loosened his grip slightly.

"I was just wondering if you were in line for the bathroom."

When Ben let go of the man's arm and hair, the guy turned around and massaged his wrist with his other hand.

Ben stepped back. "Sorry … sorry … you just startled me."

"That was pretty good," the guy said. "What was that__, some of that there judo or something?"

"I wonder," Ben uttered.

The man looked confused but before he could think about it the bathroom door opened. Ben apologized one more time before slipping inside. He locked the door behind him and walked to the sink. He splashed water on his face and then stared into the mirror wondering where he had learned that move.

When Ben exited the bathroom, the man put up his hands defensively and grinned. "Take it easy, champ."

Claire was still in the same place as she watched Ben leave the restaurant and cross the street. "Miss me?" he said. She smiled and turned toward the opening in the fence. Together they walked down the wooden steps to the sand.

A gentle breeze caressed them, and the waves crashed against the shore. Ben stared out over the water toward a blinking light on the horizon.

Claire pointed toward the light. "That's Boon Island light," she said and then pointed closer to shore. "And that's the Nubble Light."

Ben focused on the light. "Inside my empty bottle I was constructing a lighthouse while all the others were making ships."

"Who said that?" she asked.

"I have no idea," he whispered.

Claire reached over and took Ben's hand weaving her fingers in his. With their fingers interlocked, he squeezed, turned his head, and looked into her blue eyes. She blinked and for a moment she wished he would kiss her, and then she let go of his hand.

She was flirting with danger, and no matter how tempting Ben was, something about him felt wrong.

"We better be getting back," she said.

Chapter Seventeen

Ben laid the bag of Doritos in his lap and twisted the top off of the Dr. Pepper bottle. As he took a sip, his head snapped back against the headrest and his drink spilled onto his chin and down the front of his shirt. "Jesus Christ, take it easy," he said.

The man in the back seat chuckled. "Put your seatbelt on, pally, we wouldn't want anything to happen to you."

The driver looked over and agreed "Yeah, safety first."

Ben squinted to get a better look at the driver. He felt like he should know him. He took another sip of his soda and turned his neck to get a look at the man in the back seat.

"Where are we going?" Ben asked.

"He wants to know where we're going," the man in the back announced.

The driver cackled. "Where do you think we're going?"

"Did you already tell me?" Ben asked.

"Holy shit!" the driver screamed.

Ben spun his head around to see the road, but before he could make sense of what was happening he heard a loud metallic bang and the tires squealed, then he felt his head hit the roof of the car as it tumbled over and over. The driver seemed weightless as his body bounced around the car, and the man in the backseat was lying on the roof, blood exploding from his mouth. Ben felt his head hit the windshield, heard the sound of breaking glass, and suddenly everything went dark.

A moment later he heard a knocking sound.

*****

Ben opened his eyes; his heart felt like it was beating out of his chest. At first he felt like he couldn't breathe and he gasped for air.

To gain his composure, he held his breath and tried to calm down, letting his air out slowly and then breathing in through his nose and then out through his mouth again. He looked around the room; his blankets were kicked to the foot of the bed and his shirt was soaked with sweat.

Again the knocking startled him, and he realized someone was at his door.

Knock knock. "Ben," came a man's voice.

Ben swung his legs over and put his feet on the floor. "Yeah?" he answered, running his fingers through his hair.

"Breakfast is ready."

Ben recognized Cam's voice and looked at the clock. 7:45. "I'll be down in a second. Thanks, Cam."

By the time Ben got to the bottom of the stairs Mica was on his way out the door. Ben could see the waiting school bus through the screen.

"You almost missed breakfast," Mica called out as he ran by, swinging his book bag up on to his shoulder. The screen door slammed behind him.

Bob, Mildred, and Cam were already seated at the table when Ben pulled out a chair.

Bob was mopping up the last of his egg yolk with an English muffin as he nodded to Ben, and Ben nodded back.

Cam pushed his empty plate to the center of the table, leaned back, and rubbed his almost non-existent belly.

Mildred was spreading grape jelly on a piece of wheat toast. "Almost didn't make breakfast, sleepyhead," she said.

"Yeah, I don't know what that was all about," Ben answered. "I guess I was tired."

"Probably your body still recovering from whatever happened to you," Cam offered.

Ben nodded his head in agreement. "I guess."

"Haven't remembered anything?" Bob asked.

"Nothing."

Claire entered the room and picked up an empty dish off of the buffet, then took a spoon and scooped up some scrambled eggs and added two pieces of bacon and laid them on her plate. She grabbed two slices of bread out of a small wicker basket and placed them in the toaster. She looked at Ben. "Do you want me to make you a plate?"

Ben felt a little embarrassed when everyone's head turned toward him. "No, thanks. I can get it," he responded.

Ben made his plate and sat back down at the table, as did Claire. It was quiet for a moment and then there was a knock at the front door. Everyone exchanged a curious look.

"Expecting guests?" Cam asked.

"Not till tomorrow," Claire said as she went to the door.

Through the door Claire could see two men in uniform__, Chet, and one she didn't recognize.

"Good morning, Claire," Chet said.

"Good morning, Chet," Claire answered.

"Nice day," Chet offered.

The other officer lowered his brow and looked at Chet, shook his head, and then looked back at Claire. "Ma'am, I'm Officer Marx. Can we come in and speak with you for a moment?"

Ben and the others stared down the hall listening intently.

Claire pushed open the screen door to welcome them inside. "Sure," she answered. "Is something wrong?"

As the two officers walked past her into the house, she glanced outside and saw a woman across the street watching the action, as well as a man walking by on the sidewalk.

Rubberneckers.

"Nothing is wrong, Claire. We just need to speak to one of your guests," Marx answered.

Shit! Ben thought.

Chet and Marx walked into the dining room, but Marx spoke first. "Sir, can we have a word with you outside, please?"

Ben pushed his chair back from the table and started to stand when he noticed the officers were looking at Bob.

"What's this about?" Bob asked.

"Mr. Phillips," Chet insisted, "we just need to ask you a few questions."

Bob looked around the table and grinned. "I guess I must have sold someone a bad grab bar." He stood up and the officers motioned for him to go first. The three of them walked down the hall and out the front door. Chet reached for the door knob and quietly shut the door behind him.

Ben and Cam rose to their feet and quickly moved down the hall to watch through the living room window. Ben slid the curtain back carefully.

"Can you hear anything?" Cam asked.

"Shhh," Ben responded.

They watched as Bob pulled his wallet from his back pocket and showed the officers his identification. Chet shook his head yes, Bob said something, and all three laughed out loud.

Marx pulled a small piece of paper from his shirt pocket and showed it to Bob; Bob shook his head no and shrugged his shoulders.

Chet pointed down the driveway and Bob nodded yes. Both officers looked at each other and then back at Bob. Bob stuck out his hand and shook Chet's hand and then Marx. Finally Bob put his hands on his hips and watched as Chet and Marx marched back down the path and out the gate to their patrol car, but he didn't turn back toward the house until they had driven out of sight.

When Bob walked back into the house he saw Ben and Cam standing in the middle of the living room floor pretending to watch TV. "Did you get all that?" he asked the two men. Neither turned their head.

"No," Cam answered. "Couldn't hear a thing."

Bob walked back down the hall to the dining room as Cam and Ben followed.

"Everything okay?" Claire asked.

"Yeah, everything is fine," Bob answered cryptically.

"What did they want?" Mildred probed.

"They said there was a bad car accident on Shore Road, just outside of town, early Monday morning."

Mildred put her hand to her mouth. "Oh my goodness__, was anyone hurt?"

"Yeah," Bob answered. "Two guys were killed."

"What does that have to do with you?" Cam asked.

"One of the guys had my business card in his pocket," Bob answered. "The cops want me to go down to the station in a little while and look at some photos of the two guys."

"You want me to go over with you?" Cam asked.

"No, thanks. I have to head up to Kennebunkport this morning anyway. I'll stop at the police station on my way," Bob answered.

Cam nodded and reached across the table for the newspaper. "I wonder if there is anything about the accident in the newspaper."

"Well, I better get going if I'm going to stop at the police station and still make it to Kennebunkport by eleven," Bob said as he turned and made his way back down the hall.

Ben stood. "Yeah, me too. I wanted to get started on the fence."

"Better get this mess cleaned up," Claire added.

"Yeah, and I better get started on all that relaxing I have to do today," Cam said.

Mildred shook her head.

"Actually, Cam," Ben asked, "can you give me a hand with something out in the garage?"

Cam jumped at the chance to be useful. He clapped his hands together. "Sure can."

The two men walked through the front door and onto the porch just as Bob's Cadillac sped down the driveway and into the street, turning left and heading downtown.

"I hope it wasn't one of his customers," Cam said.

"Customers?" Ben asked.

"Yeah, Bob sells to hotels, motels, places like that."

"Sells what?"

"Door knobs, grab bars, shower curtain rings, things like that."

"I wondered what he did. Where's he from?"

"Not sure. I asked him that the other day and he just said, 'Down by the city.' I'm not sure which city he was talking about. Boston, maybe."

Ben walked down the steps and Cam followed. "So what did you need my help with?" Cam asked.

Ben looked back at the door to make sure no one was listening. "I'm going to tell Claire I need to run to the hardware store for more paint."

"And you need a ride?"

"Yes, but first I wanted you to take me out to where the car accident was."

"Why do you want to go out there?"

"Cam, I haven't said anything before, and I would appreciate it if you didn't say anything to anyone, but I think I was in that car accident."

Cam furrowed his brow. "What do you mean, *in* that car accident?"

Ben peered around again. "I woke up in a field on the edge of town, and when I stumbled to the road, there was broken glass scattered around, like there had been an accident and someone had already cleaned it up. I must have been laying there for hours."

"How is it you weren't still in the car when the cops and emergency crew got there?"

"I'm not sure; maybe I got out of the car after the accident or maybe I was thrown from the car. Who knows? But I need you to take me out there so I can have a look around."

"I can do that, Ben. I wanted to get the oil changed on the car before we headed out on Monday anyway. We'll go have a look around that field of yours first and then we'll go back into town and get paint and the oil changed. Maybe I'll even buy you lunch."

"Thanks, Cam, and not a word to Claire and Mildred, okay?"

Cam took his fingers and pretended to lock his lips. "Mums the word."

Chapter Eighteen

Cam and Ben sped along Shore Road in the Lacrosse but Ben's eyes were fixed past Cam through the driver's side window at the ocean. Cam gently steered the vehicle around a bend in the road, putting the water out of sight. Ben straightened his gaze back toward the road ahead.

"How long have you been staying at Claire's?" Ben asked.

Cam thought for a second. "Five days."

"You all seem pretty close."

"Yeah, I guess," Cam agreed. "This is the second time we've stayed there. We stayed for about four days when we were on our way up to Nova Scotia."

"Oh. What about Phillips? He seems like he's part of the family sometimes."

"Well I guess Bob has been staying there for a few years, since back when Claire's husband was alive. I guess twice a year his work brings him through and he stays about four or five days each time. Seems like a real nice guy."

They rounded another curve and Ben said, "Slow down; its right around here somewhere."

"Sure thing." Cam took his foot off of the gas pedal and coasted. They passed a sign and Ben looked back at it.

"I walked past that sign; it's gotta be right up here."

Cam looked along the tree line and the side of the road, not really knowing what he was looking for.

"Pull over, pull over!"

"I'll turn around up here and park on the side of the road." Cam slowed the car, eased to the right, and then made a U-turn, pulling onto the shoulder and skidding to a stop. Both men climbed out of the car.

Ben pointed at the ground. "See, here's pieces of a broken taillight and then over there there's some shattered glass."

Cam nodded in agreement and one at a time they jumped over the ditch and started walking into the field.

"Do you remember how far off the road you were?" Cam asked.

"Right up here, about thirty yards maybe."

"Let's separate … cover more area," Cam suggested as he started off in another direction.

"Good idea."

They both scanned the ground wordlessly. Ben walked in a straight line toward the coast and then turned and made his way back the same way a few feet over from his original path. Cam weaved back and forth, never taking his eyes off of the ground.

A flash caught Ben's attention, so he checked in Cam's direction to ensure he was occupied before kneeling. He picked up a shiny, metal, money clip, turning it over and flipping through the bills with his thumb. Then he jammed the clip into his front pocket.

When he got back to his feet Cam was watching him. "Find something?" he yelled.

"No. Just an old bottle," Ben yelled back. Luckily Cam bought the lie and went back to searching.

Another twenty minutes passed and Cam walked over to Ben. "Don't look like we're going to find any answers out here, pal."

"I guess you're right, Cam; it was a long shot."

The two men walked back to the car, got in, and drove back toward town. When they passed the Welcome to Dunquin Cove sign, Cam said, "I better turn off onto another street to get into town; we don't want to drive by the bed and breakfast on our way back in. If they see us they'll wonder where we've been."

"Another good idea," Ben responded. "You're pretty good at these covert operations."

"Yeah, I'm a regular James Bond."

Chapter Nineteen

Cam turned right off of Lake Street onto Main Street and took a quick left into a gas station. The yellow and red sign over the two garage doors said; LENNY'S AUTO REPAIR. Cam eased the car up to the two fuel pumps. A bell sounded as he drove over a thin black hose that ran across the property, and a short, portly man dressed in matching dark gray, Dickie shirt and pants exited the building and approached the car.

Cam pushed a button on the door and the window lowered. "You Lenny?" he asked.

The man tapped the name patch on his shirt. "Artie," he answered.

"You fellas got time to do an oil change?"

"When?"

"Now."

Artie scratched his bald head as he looked around the empty parking lot. "I think we can fit you in."

Cam opened the door and climbed out of the car. "Well, I surely appreciate that, young man."

Ben opened his door and got out.

"I left the keys in her," Cam said, slamming the door and pointing back in through the window. "Can you recommend a good place to eat?"

Artie looked up the street in one direction and then down the other. "We got the White Rose Diner over yonder," he said, pointing at a small building with light blue clap boards. "Then there's The Cove down at the end of the street; they got a bar, and if ya walk back up the way ya came, about a block, there's Lucy's. She's a mighty fine cook. That's where I usually eat when I ain't brown baggin' it."

"Thanks," Cam said.

"I could use a beer," Ben said.

Artie climbed into the car, started it up, and pulled it over in front of one of the overhead doors.

"Sounds good to me," Cam agreed. "Let's head down to that Cove place." He started walking and Ben caught up and walked alongside him.

As they walked under the yellow banner that was stretched across Main Street from one telephone pole to the other, Ben looked up and read it aloud. "Harvest Festival, October ninth through eleventh." He looked at Cam. "What exactly is a harvest festival?"

Cam shrugged. "Beats me."

Chet and Howard walked out of the White Rose Diner as Ben and Cam walked by. "Hey there, Ben," Howard called out across the street. Chet waved.

Ben waved back. "How are you gentlemen today?"

"Wonderful," Chet hollered back

"Nice day," Howard added.

Cam looked surprised. "Old friends?" he asked.

Ben just smiled.

When they came to the corner of Main and Shore, they crossed the street. As the two men passed the bakery, Ben glimpsed through the widow and caught Lita's eye. She held up a wait-a-minute finger and despite wanting to pick up his pace, Ben paused. Lita came to the door with a small white bag. "How are you today, handsome?" she asked.

"Good, Lita. You?"

She handed the bag to Ben. "Here's some bagels for you, Claire, and Mica."

"Thanks, Lita," Ben said, taking the bag. He opened it, looked inside, and inhaled the aroma. "Wow, smells great, Lita."

Lita looked Cam up and down. "Who's your handsome friend?"

"This is Cam, Cam, Lita. Cam and his wife are staying at the bed and breakfast."

"Nice to meet you, Lita," Cam said.

Lita gave a disappointed look. "A wife, huh?"

"You have a husband, Lita," Ben reminded her.

"Oh, that's right; sometimes I forget," she responded, cackling. She turned to walk back inside. "You gentlemen have a nice day."

"You too, ma'am," Cam said and they walked on.

"Howard is Lita's husband," Ben said matter-of-factly.

"Are you sure you've only been in this town for a couple of days?" Cam asked.

Ben laughed. "They're a town full of friendly people."

Cam began counting on his fingers. "Mildred and I have been here for a total of nine days and the only person I know is Lenny at the gas station, and I mistook Artie for him."

When they arrived at the restaurant, Ben grabbed the brass anchor shaped door handle and pulled the door open as Cam walked first into The Cove and took a quick look around. "Nice place," he said.

Ben nodded in agreement. "You wanna sit at the bar or at a table?"

"Let's sit at the bar," Cam replied.

As they walked to the bar, a familiar man on a stool looked over his shoulder at them. When he saw Ben he hollered out, "Hey! Well if it isn't ol' Bruce Lee."

"Another friend of yours?" Cam whispered.

"I stopped in here to use the restroom last night, and he was waiting in line behind me," Ben answered simply.

As they got to the bar the man held out his hand. "Curt Holliday."

Ben took his hand and shook. "Ben Dunning."

"I know, I know, Claire's brother-in-law," Curt replied. "With the gossip in this town, everyone knows who you are by now."

Ben pointed to Cam. "This is a friend of mine, Cam Owens."

Curt and Cam shook hands. "You guys here for lunch or just a drink."

"Both," Cam answered, as he climbed up on a stool.

"Marcia, grab these guys a menu," Curt called out to the young woman polishing glasses behind the bar.

Marcia hastily wiped her hands with a white cotton towel and pitched it under the bar. As she made her way to the other end of the bar, she pulled the rubber band from around her wrist and tied her long red hair into a pony-tail. Marcia was in her late forties, although her pale skin appeared youthful and was abundant with red freckles on her forehead and cheeks. As she reached the halfway point in the bar, she grabbed two menus off of the back bar.

Marcia smiled with perfect teeth, except for one black tooth in the right side corner of her mouth. "What can I get you gentleman?" She tossed a round cardboard coaster in front of each man.

Cam scanned the taps. "What do you got on tap there?"

Marcia recited the names. "Gritty McDuff's, Shocktop, Miller Lite, Bud Lite, New Castle Brown Ale, and Guinness."

Cam quickly pondered his choices. "I'll have the McDuff's."

"I'll have a Guinness," Ben added.

Marcia reached under the bar and pulled out two pint glasses and began filling them.

"Marcia, this here is Cam Owens and the other one is Ben Dunning," Curt introduced.

"Oh, Clay's brother," Marcia responded. She sat a glass in front of them. "Nice to meet you guys. How do you like our little town so far?"

"Very nice," Cam answered.

"Beautiful town," Ben added.

"What can I get you boys to eat?"

Cam pointed to his menu selection. "I'll have this fish sandwich with fries."

"And I'll have the lobster roll with fries," Ben said.

Marcia wrote down their orders on a guest check and disappeared through a wooden swinging door with large brass hinges. The door creaked loudly as it swung back into place.

"I have to use the restroom," Ben said, and got up from his stool. He walked down the hall and pushed open the bathroom door and went in. Taking a quick skim, he peeked under each stall for feet, and then went into the large handicapped stall.

Ben closed the door behind him and locked it. He pulled the money clip from his front pocket, pulled the money from the clip, and counted it. *On hundred, two hundred, three hundred, four hundred, four-fifty, five, five-fifty, five-seventy.* He folded the bills and shoved them back in the clip. Turning the clip over, he took out the three credit cards and driver's license. His picture was on the photograph and the name read, Wesley J. Hargreaves. The address was 37 Garden Street, Medford, Massachusetts. Ben looked at the names on the credit cards; one was Jason Stone, and the name on the other two was Charles E. Hewitt. *Is the ID fake?* He wondered. Ben replaced the cards and shoved the clip back into his pocket.

Ben opened the stall, went to the sink, and turned the water on; he washed his hands as he stared into the mirror. *Wesley Hargreaves, Jason Stone, and Charles Hewitt.* He wondered which name he looked like most.

Cam was in a friendly argument with Curt, Marcia, and another man sitting at the bar. Ben wasn't sure what they were talking about, but he heard the words "Boston," "money," and "series" as he approached and climbed back on his stool.

"Who do you like?" Marcia asked.

"Never was much of a sports guy," Ben answered. He wondered if he never knew much about sports or if it had something to do with the accident.

Ding! "Order up," came a deep voice from the kitchen.

As they dug into their food, Ben began to wonder who Wesley Hargreaves really was, and what kind of trouble he'd gotten himself into.

Chapter Twenty

"That was good," Cam commented as he and Ben walked along the sidewalk back toward Lenny's garage.

Ben was using his finger as a toothpick. "Sure was. Maybe one too many beers though." His fingernail got what it was after and flicked it into the street.

"Should hold me over till dinner," Cam added. His face was red and he was grinning for no apparent reason other than a slight case of alcohol-induced stupor.

Ben looked at the buildings across the street as they walked. Right across from Lita's was an ice cream shop and next door to that was a mom and pop grocery store. Ben had an idea and turned to Cam. "Hey, why don't we run in there and grab some steaks for dinner. I saw a grill in the garage, back at Claire's; we could all have dinner together tonight … I mean, if you don't have any plans."

"Sounds like a great idea to me," Cam agreed, and they both turned and made their way across the street.

When they got to the glass doors of the grocery, Ben pushed but the door didn't budge. Cam pointed at the small sign that said "pull" and then pushed on the other door and went in. "You must have forgot how to read, too," Cam said with a chuckle.

Ben laughed. "Maybe I *wasn't* in an accident; maybe I'm just a moron."

The two men were still laughing when they found the meat counter. Ben eyed the Delmonico's while Cam looked over the strip steaks.

"We'll have three of these Delmonico's and three of those strips," Ben said.

The thick man behind the counter said, "Comin right up, pal." He slid the glass doors open on the back of the cooler and reached his short hairy arms in to grab the meat. "You gentlemen staying here in town?" he asked as he stacked three of the steaks, one on top of the other, on the scales.

"Staying over at the Colsome House," Cam answered.

The butcher wrapped the strip steaks in white paper and taped the package closed. "Oh, Claire's place. Nice place she got there."

"Sure is. This is the second time we've stayed there," Cam agreed.

The butcher looked up through the glass at Ben as he retrieved the Delmonico's. "You Clay's brother?"

Ben nodded. "Yes … yes, I am."

The butcher stood, wiped his hand on the front of the apron that was stretched across his huge belly, and stuck his arm over the counter. "Ben, isn't it?"

"Yes," Ben answered, shaking his hand.

"John," the butcher said.

Ben nodded toward Cam. "This here is Cam."

John and Cam shook hands and then John went back to his task of preparing the meat. When he was finished wrapping the second package he wrote the price on each in black marker and slid them across the counter.

"Well, it was nice meeting you guys. Enjoy your dinner and tell Claire I said hey."

"Will do," Ben said as he grabbed the steaks.

"We're gonna need some beer," Cam said.

"Great idea," Ben answered, pointing at Cam.

Halfway down the beer aisle Cam took hold of an abandoned grocery cart and put the steaks in the seat. "We passed some corn on the cob that looked pretty good too."

"How about some of these salt potatoes?" Ben asked.

"Sounds good."

"I'm starving just thinking about it."

Ben laid them in the cart.

*****

"Forty-four dollars and seventeen cents," said the young girl at the cash register.

Cam reached for his wallet.

"Let me get this," Ben said, pulling the money clip from his pocket.

Cam lowered his brow; he looked confused but said nothing.

The girl packed the groceries into two brown paper bags, took Ben's money, handed him back his change, and told the two men to have a nice day.

Back out on the sidewalk, Cam asked, "Where did you get the money?"

"I found it lying in the field, Cam."

"It must be yours … right? It can't be a coincidence that you found a wallet in the same field you woke up in two days earlier."

"That's what I thought."

"Was there a driver's license or any other form of identification?"

"There was a driver's license and three credit cards."

"Well … then … what's your name?"

"I have no idea."

"What was the name on the cards?"

"There were three different names."

Cam looked puzzled. "Do you think they're stolen or fake names?"

"I don't know. I was going to Google the names when we got back to Claire's__, see if anything comes up."

"You're on your own with that there computer stuff," Cam stated, scratching his head. "Computers just ain't my thing."

*****

When Ben and Cam arrived back at Lenny's Garage, Artie was backing the Lacrosse out of one of the bays. He backed up to the pumps, threw it in drive, and then swung the car around to the side of the building and parked. Artie climbed out of the car, slammed the door, and then pulled the red rag from his back pocket to wipe the smudges off of the door handle. As he rounded the back of the vehicle he looked up and noticed the men walking toward him. "Just finished her up," he said.

"Perfect timing. What do I owe you?" Cam asked.

"Are ya payin with cash or credit card?"

"Cash," Cam answered, knowing it would get him a little better price at a small garage like Lenny's.

"Twenty-five bucks should do it."

Cam pulled his wallet from his back pocket, took out a twenty and a ten and handed it to Artie. "Good enough," he said.

Artie folded the bills and shoved them into his shirt pocket. "Thanks," Artie said. "Not many out of towners tip, but this makes two days in a row … only you two guys are a lot friendlier than that guy yesterday."

Cam laughed. "At least he tipped ya."

"Yeah, I guess. I think he only tipped me because he felt bad for yelling at me."

"Why did he yell at you?" Ben asked.

"Funny thing," Artie began. "The guy pulls in here in a big black Cadillac—" Ben and Cam exchange a knowing look then returned their attention to Artie. "He's almost riding on the rim, mud and grass all over the car. Without me even telling him to, he pulls right into the garage. I come walking out the front door and he says, 'Hey, buddy, I need you to fix that flat and then wash my car.' He tosses me the keys and starts walking down the street."

"Where did the yelling come in?" Ben asked.

Artie pointed at the garage. "Well, he had pulled his car into the bay without the lift, so instead of backing it out and pulling into the other bay, I just opened his trunk and took out his jack to change the tire. After I changed the tire I backed the car out front here to wash it. When I was done I ran back in the garage to grab his jack. I was bent over putting it back in the trunk when all a sudden the guy grabs me from behind, spins me around, and grabs ahold of the front of my shirt with his fists. Guy almost lifted me off the ground! Scared the shit outta me, excuse my French. Then he gets right in my face and says, 'Who the hell told you you could open the trunk?'"

Cam just let out a breathy, "Wow."

"Yeah, wow," Artie repeated. "When I told him I was just putting the jack back he calmed down, straightened my shirt, and apologized."

"Was there something in the trunk you weren't supposed to see?" Ben asked.

"Who knows," Artie answered. "I didn't notice anything back there."

"The guy say where he was from?" Cam asked.

"The plates said Massachusetts," Artie answered.

"Did ya get a name?" Ben asked.

"Nope, and he paid in cash … fifty dollar tip."

Ben thought about describing Bob to Artie just to make sure that it was him, but then decided not to. He hadn't noticed if Bob's plates were from Massachusetts or not but he would surely be checking tonight.

Cam and Ben put the groceries in the back seat, climbed into the car, and drove away.

When they were headed back down Shore Road, Cam turned to Ben. "I wonder why Bob is so jumpy."

Ben responded, "I wonder what's in that trunk."

Chapter Twenty-One

It was almost one o'clock by the time Ben and Cam walked through the front doors of the Colsome House, grocery bags in hand.

"Looks like you boys did a little shopping while you were out," Mildred commented from the sofa. She had a *Country Living* magazine, face down and open, lying in her lap. Her reading glasses hung from a thin chain around her neck, and her feet were propped up on an ottoman that matched the sofa. Cam knew by the look in her eyes that his wife had been doing more sleeping than reading.

"Picked up a couple steaks for dinner tonight," Ben answered.

"We thought it would be a nice night to cook out and all eat dinner together," Cam added.

Mildred nodded in agreement with a smile. "That sounds like a great idea."

"That's what I said," Cam agreed.

Ben reached for the bag Cam was holding. "I'll take these into the kitchen."

Cam said, "Thanks," and joined his wife on the couch. He immediately reached for the television remote control.

"It was nice without the TV on," Mildred offered.

Cam ignored her and pointed the remote at the television anyway.

"Nice and quiet," she added.

Cam pressed the big red button marked power.

"Don't you like it quiet and peaceful?" Mildred asked.

"Why, yes, I do," Cam stated, pointing the remote at his wife and pressing the mute button.

"Very funny. I just meant maybe we could sit here and just talk."

Cam looked at the remote with a confused expression and then shook it. Pointing it at Mildred once again, he pressed the mute button several times. "Batteries must be dead." He aimed it back at the television and flipped slowly through the channels until he came to an old rerun of *Bonanza*. He laid the remote on the couch next to him and folded his arms across his chest.

Mildred settled her glasses back on her nose, picked up the magazine, and began reading an article about painting old milk cans and turning them into planters.

*****

Ben was putting the packages of meat into the refrigerator when Claire rounded the corner and came up the cellar steps with a laundry basket in her hands. "Watcha got there?" she asked.

"A few steaks," Ben answered. He pulled the salt potatoes from one of the bags and showed Claire. "And some potatoes."

Claire took the potatoes from Ben. "Mica loves salt potatoes."

Ben pointed at the bag on the counter. "Got some corn on the cob too."

"What's the occasion?"

"Cam and I thought we could cook out. I saw a grill in the garage."

"That old thing__, I don't even know if it works."

Ben folded the bag he had emptied. "Do you keep these for anything?"

"Anything like what?"

Ben shrugged his shoulders. "I don't know."

Claire took the bag and stuck it in the cabinet under the sink. "It will be right here if you need it for anything."

"Thanks," Ben said gruffly, and went toward the cellar steps. "I'll go out and see if I can get that grill started."

Claire picked up her basket of laundry and went back to her chores.

When Ben got to the garage door, he grabbed the handle and tugged, but it didn't budge. He yanked it again, this time putting everything he had into it. Again the door didn't budge, but the screws holding the handle ripped through the rotted wood, sending Ben tumbling backwards into the driveway, handle still in hand. "Sonofabitch," he whispered and threw the handle at the door.

Climbing to his feet, he dusted off his ass and looked around to see if anyone had seen his fall. When he was satisfied that his act of clumsiness had gone undetected, he returned to the door. Grabbing the locking mechanism, he tried to lift the door once more, and the door rose about two inches and jammed into place. He let go of his grip and the door stayed where it was. *Dammit.*

Going around to the side entrance, which was a crooked wooden door, he took hold of the knob and turned. Predictability the door didn't move. Ben threw his shoulder into the door ripping it from its rusted hinges. Taking hold of the loose door, he leaned it up against the garage wall and returned to the overhead door. Inspecting the track on each side of the door, he located the problem__, a four foot piece of two-by-four had fallen against the door and wedged itself between the wheel and track. He yanked the board from its position and placed it on the floor.

Ben wiggled his fingers under the garage door and lifted it above his head. It squeaked and squealed as he pushed it into its upright position. When he let go, the door began to close on its own, but he shoved it back and searched for a longer two by four. Finding one about six feet long, he placed it next to the track, under the edge of the door, and pulled the door down to rest on top of the board. "There," he said triumphantly and released a long sigh.

Flipping on the light switch, Ben walked to the back of the garage to retrieve the grill. The plastic wheels wobbled and the metal frame of the grill swayed back and forth as he dragged it out of the garage.

Ben lifted the lid and looked inside.

"How's everything going out here?" Cam called out from the driveway.

Ben peeked under the grill at the propane tank and mumbled, "I broke the garage door and ripped the side door off its hinges just getting this thing into the driveway. I can't wait to see what happens when I try to light it."

Cam laughed and joined Ben in front of the grill. "Any gas in the tank?"

Ben lifted the tank. "Feels pretty light."

Cam walked into the garage as Ben inspected the grill. Pointing at the two by four holding up the door, Cam said, "Nice door stop."

"Yeah, be careful with that; one of the springs is broken and that door is about a hundred and fifty pounds."

Cam walked under the door, and after a few minutes he hollered, "Unhook that tank."

"Why?"

"Just unhook it," Cam answered. He exited the garage with an old bag of charcoal briquettes in one hand and a plastic jug of lighter fluid in the other. "Problem solved. We'll just turn the gas grill into a charcoal grill."

"You're a regular old MacGyver."

Cam shot Ben a look. "You can't remember who you are, but you remember MacGyver?"

Ben looked confused. "That is funny," he answered. "I just had this memory of sitting on the floor watching television. It was like a flash in my head ... like a dream. I could see myself sitting there; I must have been about eleven or twelve years old."

"Anything else?"

Ben scratched his head. "No, nothing."

"Maybe everything will slowly start coming back."

Ben furrowed his brow. "Yeah, maybe it will."

"You seem like you don't want to remember."

"It's not that I don't want to, it's ... it's just what if I don't like what I remember?"

"What do you mean?"

"The car crash, the money clip__, what if I don't like who I was?"

Cam placed his hand on Ben's shoulder. "You're a good man, Ben. I've gotten to know you over these past few days. You couldn't have been that much different before."

Ben looked back at the house and thought of Claire. "What if I'm married or have a family?"

"And now you have feelings for Claire."

Ben hated the answer to this question, but he couldn't deny it. "Yes."

Chapter Twenty-Two

A gentle breeze blew, trying it's best to unhook the last remaining leaves of summer. Mica struggled to help Cam move the picnic table closer to the grill and then went back for the benches. Mildred spread a red-and-white-checkered tablecloth over the table.

Claire came out of the back door carrying the radio from the kitchen. "Mica set this on the table and grab the extension cord out of the garage so I can plug it in."

Ben looked around the yard at everyone and then focused his eyes on the flames that danced among the charcoal and wondered if his old life could possibly be any better than his new one.

"Almost ready?" Cam asked.

"Just about," Ben answered somberly.

Cam slapped him on the back. "I'll grab the steaks."

Mica plugged in the radio and switched it on. A female voice began telling the group that it was sixty-eight degrees, there was a slight breeze out of the east, and the weather was going to be perfect for this weekend's events during the Harvest Fest, then Jimmy Buffett began singing "Come Monday." Ben was surprised when Cam, plate of meat in hand, began singing along, and then even more surprised when he himself joined in.

Cam shot him a grin as he crossed the yard and the two men continued their duet. Cam sat the plate at the edge of the table and went back into the house. When he returned he was carrying a small cooler, which he sat on the ground at the end of the table. Opening the lid he jammed his hand into the ice, pulling out two long neck bottles of Bud-Lite. Cam handed one bottle to Ben and then opened the other and gave it to his wife. He reached back into the cooler and retrieved one for himself; he twisted off the cap and took a long-needed gulp. "Ahhh."

Ben heard the sound of tires on pavement; it was Bob Phillips. He brought his Cadillac to a halt at the edge of the house, opened the door, and got out. He looked at the group, clearly wondering what was going on.

"I hope you're hungry, Bob. I got a steak here for ya," Ben called out.

"And a beer," Cam added, holding his own bottle in the air.

Bob opened the rear door of his car and took out his briefcase. "Sounds like that's just what I need," he said. He walked around to the back of the car and, pointing his keys at the trunk pushed a button and the trunk popped open. He placed the briefcase inside the trunk and closed it. Cam and Ben looked at each other and then back at Bob.

Cam reached back inside the cooler and grabbed another beer. "Here ya go," he said, placing it on the table next to the radio.

Bob walked across the driveway to the back door. "I'm going to run up to my room and put on something a little more comfortable," he said.

Cam whispered to Ben, "Probably one of those Tony Soprano track suits."

Ben looked confused.

"Never mind," Cam said.

"I think the coals are ready," Ben said. Cam picked up the plate of meat and handed it to Ben. Ben placed each steak, one at a time, on the grill, and basked in the sound of the hot grill searing the meat.

"Smells good already," Cam said.

When Bob exited the back door he was wearing dark blue jeans that looked like they had never been washed or worn, a white sweatshirt with a large red B on the front, and white sneakers. Bob glanced over at Claire who wore a large grin on her face.

"What?" Bob asked.

"Nothing."

"It must be something; you've got a huge smile on your face."

"I've known you for years, Bob, and this is the first time I've seen you in anything but a suit."

Bob smiled and headed toward his awaiting beer. "Just felt like getting comfortable." He grabbed his beer, twisted off the top, pitched it on the table, and took a sip. "That's good after a long day."

"How did everything go down at the police station this morning?" Claire asked, which got everyone's attention.

"Good, I guess. They had me look at a couple of snapshots of the two guys who were killed in the car accident."

"Was it anybody you knew?" Cam asked.

"Nope, never seen either one of them before."

"You know why they might have had your business card on them?" Mildred asked.

"No idea."

"Probably picked it up somewhere they had stayed," Ben offered.

"Maybe."

Just then Mica came walking out of the garage with a baseball and two gloves. "Ben, you wanna play catch?" he asked.

Ben looked down at the steaks. "I gotta co—"

"Go play catch with the boy," Cam interrupted, taking the fork from Ben.

"Yeah, okay," Ben agreed.

Mica handed one of the gloves to Ben and ran to the other side of the yard. Ben slid his fingers into the glove and stared into the webbing.

Mica held up his glove. "Throw it." Ben threw the ball into the air. Mica backed up a few steps and the ball dropped into his glove.

"Nice catch," Ben called out and looked to Claire, who was watching him, but she averted her glance quickly when their eyes met. Mica tossed the ball back, and after a perfect arc it met the web of Ben's glove with a smack.

Bob took a seat at the picnic table and nursed his beer. He looked over at Cam and said, "I've got a few Cubans up in my room that I picked up in Nova Scotia last month. I'll bring them down after dinner."

"That would be great." Cam thought for a second. "I haven't had a Cuban cigar since we sold the ranch. Had an old boy who used to bring a few to me every year when he came from Canada down through Montana."

Claire fetched a couple of folding chairs from the garage and sat them near the table. Mildred sat in one and put her feet up on one of the picnic table benches; she tipped her head back and took a nice long swig of her beer.

"I think these steaks are just about done, Claire how's those potatoes and corn coming along?"

Claire was just about to sit down. "Just waiting on you," she answered.

Mildred got up and set her bottle on the table. "I'll give you a hand, sweetie."

Mildred followed Claire through the back door, then the two quickly returned. Mildred carried a large bowl containing the salt potatoes and Claire was holding a platter with the ears of corn neatly piled high.

"I'll bring out some melted butter for the potatoes, and I made some coleslaw," Claire announced, setting the plate of corn in the middle of the picnic table.

Cam took the steaks off the grill one at a time and stacked them on the platter.

"Can I help with anything?" Bob asked.

"No, dear, only a couple more things," Mildred answered.

Bob got up anyway and returned with the bowl of coleslaw.

When the table was set, everyone took a seat, Mildred between Cam and Bob on one side of the table and Mica between Ben and Claire on the other.

Cam took a steak for himself and then passed the plate to his wife. Bob grabbed an ear of corn and then passed that plate across the table to Claire, who took a piece for herself and then one for Mica.

Ben looked over the table at Bob. "Did the cops tell you anything about the accident?"

"No. I asked a couple of questions but they told me they weren't at liberty to discuss an ongoing investigation," Bob answered.

"Questions like what?" Cam asked.

"I just wondered if they had any identification on them, and what kind of car they were driving … you know, things like that," Bob responded with a mouth full of corn.

"That's an awful nice car you got there," Cam said.

"Thanks."

"That a company car or is it yours?"

"She's mine; picked her up in Florida in the spring."

"That where you're from … Florida?" Ben asked.

Bob smiled. "No."

"Boston?" Cam asked.

Bob laid his ear of corn on his plate, put his elbows on the table, and interlocked his fingers in front of him. "I was born in Inglewood, New Jersey, I grew up in a town called Norwood. When I was sixteen I kicked the shit out of my abusive stepfather and went to live with an uncle in Brooklyn. Now I live in Boston. Have no children. Five years ago, my wife of ten years was run down in a crosswalk on her way to have lunch with friends, but they never caught the guy." Bob paused at the end of his story and looked around the table; all eyes were on him. He turned back to Cam. "Does that tell you everything you need to know about me, Cam?"

Cam cleared his throat. "Just making conversation, Bob. I didn't mean to upset you."

Bob's stare was blank. "I'm not upset."

Claire tried to change the subject. "Great steaks, Cam, thanks."

"Thank Ben, Claire; he bought them."

Bob lowered his brow. "You paid for them?"

Ben stuttered. "Well ... I ... uh ..."

"I loaned him a few bucks," Cam cut in. "So he paid for them."

Bob sipped his beer, staring intently over the bottle at Ben. "That was very nice of you, Ben."

Ben nodded.

"Well, whoever treated, it was a very nice meal," Mildred chimed in.

"Yes it was," Claire agreed.

"I think I'll grab those cigars," Bob said. "Perfect ending to a perfect meal."

When Bob went through the back door, the others looked around the table at each other. Claire spoke first. "I just learned more about Bob in the last few minutes than I have in the last few years."

"Seems like a private guy," Mildred pointed out.

"Yeah, a little too private," Cam added.

"Oh Cam, calm down," Mildred ordered. "I think maybe you have been watching way too many cop shows on the idiot box."

"I don't know; there's something not quite right about that guy. He seems different in the last couple of days."

Claire pointed her chin toward Mica. "Cam, please."

Cam put up his hands. "I'm just saying," he said, and looked to Ben for his support. Ben just smiled and took a drink of his beer.

Mildred knew what Cam was up to and said, "Don't get Ben mixed up in your harebrained ideas."

Claire stood and started clearing the table, and Mildred followed suit.

"This would be a nice night for a fire," Cam exclaimed.

Claire picked up the plate of stripped corn cobs. "There's a little metal fireplace behind the garage, and a few pieces of firewood too."

Cam got up from the table and walked around the back of the garage. Turned on its side and leaning against the garage was a rusted outdoor fireplace, and next to it were about fifteen or twenty pieces of firewood that had been cut years ago.

When Cam returned he was carrying an armful of firewood. "I don't think we have to worry whether or not the wood is dry enough."

Ben retrieved the fireplace and Cam began stacking it with the wood, starting with the smaller pieces and then topped the pile with the larger. When Cam was finished, Ben squirted the wood with the lighter fluid.

Bob returned with a lighter and three cigars in his hand. "Oh perfect," Cam said. "Can I borrow that lighter for a second?" Bob handed him the lighter and he lit the wood.

Bob handed a cigar to Ben who bit off the tip and rolled it in his mouth until the end was moist. Cam tossed him the lighter. Ben flipped open the lid of the Zippo, thumbed the wheel, and held the flame to the end of the stogie. He slowly turned the cigar as he drew in the smoke. He held the smoke in his mouth for a moment and then blew it out through his mouth and nose. "Nice," he proclaimed, tossing the lighter to Bob. Indeed, a perfect ending to a perfect meal.

Chapter Twenty-Three

Mica sat on the ground with his legs crossed, his baseball glove on one hand and with the other he tossed the ball into the air a few feet, over and over again, catching it in the glove each time. In one of the lawn chairs directly behind him sat Ben, and in a chair to Ben's left was Bob, and to his right, Cam. The only light was the flickering flames of the fire.

The men smoked the last few inches of their Cuban cigars, blowing smoke into the cool evening air above their heads. The radio had been turned down and Gordon Lightfoot could be softly heard singing "Sundown."

"How old do I gotta be to have a cigar?" Mica asked, pulling the ball from the glove's webbing and throwing it back into the air.

"I was fifteen," Bob answered.

"I was eleven," Cam chimed in. "Puked my guts out."

"You have to be eighteen," Ben said.

"Why do I have to be eighteen?"

"That's the rules," Bob answered.

"You weren't eighteen."

Cam chuckled. "Times were different back then, my boy, times were different."

"I probably won't wait," Mica declared. "It looks fun."

"It is fun," Cam agreed. "But don't tell your mother I said so."

"Don't worry, I know the difference between guy talk and girl talk."

"Ya do, huh?" Ben asked.

"What happens at the fire, stays at the fire," Cam chuckled.

"Mica!" Claire hollered from the back door. "It's time for you to come in and get ready for bed."

"But we only have half a day tomorrow."

Claire crossed her arms. "I don't care if you have half a day, you still have to get up at the same time."

"But, Mom," Mica whined in defiance. "us guys are talking."

"Well, you're done talking. Let's go. Tell everyone goodnight"

Mica slowly climbed to his feet. "Sorry, guys, I gotta go in." As he passed the group, he put his hand on Ben's arm. "Will you still be here tomorrow?"

"Yeah. Why?"

"I was wondering if you could come down to the school and pick me up tomorrow. I'm staying after to work on the float for the parade and I'll miss the bus home. You don't have to if you don't wanna. I just thought if … um, you … uh … were bored or something."

Claire heard her son's request but said nothing as she stood in the doorway holding open the screen door waiting for Ben's answer.

Ben rested his hand on Mica's shoulder. "Sure, I can do that. Maybe you could even let me have a look at that float you're building."

Mica's face lit up. "Yeah, I'll show ya. It's really cool. It looks like a pirate ship and there's a big whee—"

"Come on, Mica, say your goodnights and let's go," Claire summoned once again.

Mica threw his arms around Ben's neck. "I'll see you in the morning," he said, then ran for the back door. Stopping halfway, he spun around. "Oh yeah, good night, Mr. Phillips and Mr. Owens."

Bob and Cam yelled good night as Mica disappeared through the door.

"Good kid," Cam said.

Bob nodded his head in agreement and flicked the last of his cigar into the fire. "I guess I better head up too. I have to drive all the way up to Rockland tomorrow." He stood with a groan. "I'll see you gentlemen tomorrow."

"Yeah, I think I'll call it a night too," Cam announced. He rose to his feet. He looked down at Ben. "You comin' in?"

"I'll be in in a minute, Cam. I'll finish up this cigar while the fire dies down."

"That boy's really takin' a likin' to ya."

"I guess."

"He's gonna hate when ya have to leave."

"I know, Cam."

Cam patted Ben on the shoulder and went in the house.

Ben sat alone staring into the fire pit, watching the last of the glowing embers dance in the darkness. Leaning forward, he picked up a small piece of wood and flung it onto the fire. He watched the embers as they shot skyward and twirled in the breeze. He picked up another piece and pitched it in with the other.

He took one last drag on his cigar, held the smoke in his mouth for a second, and then slowly let it escape. When the last of the smoke rolled over his tongue, he threw the cigar into the fire and took a sip of his beer.

"Last to leave the party?" Claire's voice broke the silence, startling Ben.

"Jeeze, I didn't hear you walk up," he responded.

Claire sat in the chair next to Ben and scooted it closer to the fire. She held her hands out in front of her, and then rubbed them together. "Starting to cool off a little." She drew her cardigan tighter around her and buttoned it halfway up.

"Yes, it is."

"Mica says you're going to pick him up after school tomorrow."

"Oh, yeah, I probably should have asked you first, but—"

"No, that's fine. He's very excited."

"He's a great kid."

"Thanks."

Ben sat quietly for a moment trying to think of something to talk about. "I was going to take a closer look at that garage door tomorrow, see what it needs to fix it."

"I would like to have a new one installed," she responded. "But they wanted an arm and a leg."

"Well, I'll fix it for now and then later if you want—" He paused, suddenly realizing he was referring to the future. A future that held what, exactly? He didn't know.

The pause wasn't quick enough and Claire shot him a look. "Later? There's no later."

"I just meant … that …"

For the first time Claire grasped just how she would feel if he left. She stood. "You have a whole other life somewhere, Ben. In a few days you will be leaving. You can't stay here forever." She started to walk away but Ben grabbed her arm.

"Claire, wait."

She turned back and Ben stood up, facing her. "Wait for what, Ben?"

Ben's grip remained steadfast, holding her arm in one hand and placing the other behind her head as he pulled her toward him and kissed her. She leaned back and stared into his eyes and then hastily pressed her lips against his.

"You kids coming in?" came Mildred's voice from the back door.

The two parted swiftly and saw Mildred walking in their direction. "We were just … I mean, we were going to … we'll be right in." Claire's voice cracked as she spoke.

Mildred grinned wryly. "I'm sorry, did I interrupt something?" Mildred asked as she opened the cooler and pulled out a bottle of beer.

Claire straightened her sweater and ran her hands through her hair. "Nope, we were just picking up."

"Looked like someone was getting picked up," Mildred chuckled.

Cam called through the upstairs window, "Did you check if there's any beer left?"

"I'm coming__, keep your pants on," Mildred hollered back as she headed back toward the house.

When the door slammed behind Mildred, Ben was still smiling widely. "That was embarrassing."

Claire smiled back sheepishly. "I haven't been caught making out in a long time. I better make sure Mica is in bed," she said, backing up toward the door. "Good night, Ben."

"Good night, Claire."

Halfway to the door Claire stopped and ran back to Ben. Throwing her arms around his shoulders, she kissed him once more, then spun around and bolted for the door.

Ben turned back to the fire and sat down in his chair, sipping his beer. He didn't realize he was still smiling until some of his beer dripped out of the corner of his mouth and onto his shirt. With the back of his hand he wiped it away, yet nothing would wipe away the excitement he felt.

Chapter Twenty-Four

It was one in the morning when Ben's half empty-beer bottle slipped from his fingers and hit the ground with a thud, startling him awake. The fire had long since burned out and only a slight red glow in the ash remained. Ben slouched down in the chair, and when he straightened up every muscle in his body felt sore. He leaned over, picking up the beer bottle and setting it on the dew-covered tablecloth. He stood and looked back at the house, all of the windows were dark except for a dim light in the kitchen. The radio played "House of the Rising Sun"; Ben reached over and shut it off before going inside.

Ben locked the back door behind him and made his way through the kitchen and into the dining room. He tried to walk as carefully and as quietly as he could, attempting to keep the wooden floor from creaking beneath his feet, but it was no use. When he got to the top of the stairs, he overheard a mumbled voice. He put his hand on the door knob to his room and turned it. Even the click of the cylinder seemed loud in the quiet night, and a moment later the talking stopped. Ben pushed his door open and the voice resumed.

Leaving his door open, Ben backed into the hall and sidestepped quietly to Bob's door. Craning his neck, he pressed his ear to the door. Bob was trying to whisper, but he was obviously angry, which piqued Ben's interest.

"I don't know who he is ... how the hell would I know? I'll take care of it ... I don't know ... he says he doesn't remember anything ... Let me put it this way__, if any of your cronies show their faces in this town I'll put a bullet in their heads and then one in yours. Do you think I won't?" Bob threatened. *"It's under contr—"* Ben pulled back from the door an inch and the floor creaked at the shift in weight.

Bob stopped mid-sentence and a minute later his doorknob turned. The door cracked open and Bob stuck his eye up to the opening.

Ben's door clicked shut.

Bob opened his door the rest of the way and looked down the hall in one direction and then the other. When he saw no one, he gently closed his door. "I'll call you back tomorrow," he said and hung up his phone.

Chapter Twenty-Five

It was eight o'clock Thursday morning when Ben backed Claire's mini-van out of the garage and parked it in the driveway. He returned to the garage, picked up a wooden step ladder that hung from two sixteen penny nails on the garage wall, and stood it up under the broken door spring. Walking to the back of the garage, he searched the peg board for some pliers and an adjustable wrench. Finding what he needed, he climbed up on the third step of the ladder and began removing the safety cable that ran from one end of the track, through the spring, to the other end of the track. When the cable was removed, he unhooked the spring and dropped it to the ground below him.

"What's on the agenda for today?" Cam asked as the spring rolled across the floor and stopped at his feet.

"I thought I would run down to the hardware store and get a couple new springs for this door," Ben responded.

"We *could* do that," Cam said.

Ben laid the wrench on the ladder tray and eyed Cam. "What do you mean, 'We *could* do that'?"

"I mean, we *could* fix the garage door, or we *could* jump in my car and follow ol' Bob when he leaves for," Cam made finger quotes, "work."

"What if he's just going to," Ben made finger quotes, "work?"

"Then we'll know. But if he doesn't go to work then we'll know that."

Ben thought about the conversation he overheard the night before. He wondered if he should tell Cam. *Cam seems to be able to keep a secret*, he thought. He decided to wait and if it turned out that Bob did have something to hide, he could always tell Cam what he overheard at that point. Ben nodded. "Yeah, we could follow him."

"Good. Now let's go in and get some breakfast. We'll come back out here and pretend to work on the door and then when we hear his car leave we'll follow."

Ben climbed down from the ladder. "What are you going to tell your wife?"

"I'll tell her we have to run to the hardware store."

"Okay, but I have to be at the school by two-thirty to pick up Mica."

"I thought he only had half a day."

"A half a day of school but he's working on the float after school."

"No problem," Cam assured him as they walked in through the back door.

Mildred was already sitting at the dining room table spreading orange marmalade on a piece of toast when Cam and Ben entered the room and began making their plates. She held the newspaper open in front of her and was reading down through the list of events for the Harvest Fest. "The parade starts at five o'clock tomorrow night," she said.

"We can't miss that," Cam answered.

"There's a 5k Saturday morning at nine," Mildred continued.

Cam looked at Ben and said, "If you ever see me running down the street you better start running too, because a herd of something big is chasing me."

Ben laughed as he scooped scrambled eggs onto his plate.

"You were quite the runner in school, Cam, and you know it," Mildred argued. "Some of your records still stand."

"Yeah, well that was fifty-some years ago."

Mildred continued reading aloud. "Craft fair starts at eleven Saturday and there's going to be rides in the park Saturday and Sunday."

"If you're going to read the paper to us this morning why don't you head on over to the sports page," Cam complained.

Mildred shot him a nasty look over the top of the paper and continued on, reading to herself.

"I'm gonna run Ben over to the hardware store in a bit so he can pick up new springs for that garage door, you need anything down town?" Cam asked his wife.

"Maybe I'll tag along with you boys."

Cam and Ben looked at each other quickly and then back at Mildred. "Oh, you don't have to do that," Cam stated.

"I don't mind."

Ben jumped in. "It'll probably be pretty boring."

"That's okay, I'll walk over to the drug store while you guys are in the hardware store. I have to pick up a couple things."

"I can pick them up for you," Cam offered.

Mildred lowered the newspaper and her brow. "Sounds like you two don't want me to go. What's going on?"

Cam stuttered. "I ... uh ... we ..."

"We met a couple guys at the bar yesterday when we had lunch. We got to talking to them and they invited us back today for a couple drinks and to play cards," Ben said.

Mildred picked the paper back up. "Well, why didn't you just say so."

Cam breathed a sigh of relief.

Ben heard the stairs creak one by one and he knew Bob was on his way down. He looked down the hall and could see Bob's fingers as they grabbed the railing.

"How are you folks this morning?" Bob said as he made his way to the buffet.

"Good," everyone said in unison.

"You?" Mildred asked.

Bob dropped two pieces of bread into the toaster. "I think I drank one too many of those beers last night, got a slight headache this morning."

"Where ya heading today?" Cam asked.

Bob pulled his toast from the toaster and began buttering it. "Heading up to Sanford today."

"Hotel?" Cam asked.

"It's a nursing home," Bob answered.

"You want me to grab a couple of aspirins for you, Bob?" Mildred asked.

"That would be great, Mildred. I don't have any."

"Grab me a couple too," Cam said.

"Too many beers?" Bob asked with a smile.

"No, the doctor says I'm supposed to take one a day."

Bob poured himself a cup of coffee. "How late did you stay out there, Ben?"

"I came in around one, I think."

"One?" Bob repeated.

"Yeah. I didn't wake you did I?"

"Nope. I fell right to sleep the second my head hit the pillow."

Mildred returned with the aspirins. "Here ya go." She handed Bob's to him and then Cam his.

Bob tossed his to the back of his throat and took a gulp of his coffee. "Thanks Mildred." He placed a napkin in his hand and dropped his toast on top of it, then picked his coffee back up in the other hand. "Well, I better get going."

Cam shoveled the last of his breakfast quickly into his mouth. "Yeah, we better get going too. Come on, Ben that door ain't gonna fix itself."

"You boys have fun," Mildred said, keeping her eyes on the newspaper. "Pick up toothpaste and shampoo!" she hollered as the back door slammed shut.

Cam pressed the button on his key chain unlocking the car doors. "Didn't he say last night that he was going to Rockland today?"

"Yes, he did," Ben answered.

"And today he says Sanford."

The two men climbed into Cam's car and began backing down the driveway speculating why Bob would lie, and what he would possibly be lying about.

Chapter Twenty-Six

Cam eased his car to a halt at the stop sign on the corner of Shore Road and Main Street. Ben looked down the street to the right toward The Cove while Cam looked up the street toward Lenny's garage. "Did ya see which way he went?" Cam asked.

"I thought he turned right," Ben answered.

"I think that was his car that took a left."

"We were too far away, I couldn't tell which car was his."

"I think it's right."

"Then go right."

The car behind them honked. Cam looked in his rearview mirror at the man frantically waving his arms in the air. "Hold your horses, asshole," he said and slowly turned onto Main Street.

They drove by Lenny's Garage, where Cam took his foot off the gas while the two of them inspected Lenny's property for a clue. Artie was walking out of the garage, saw them, and waved. Ben and Cam waved back. When they came to Lake Street Cam slowed the car again as they looked up and down the street, and then did the same at the next street.

"Dammit! I think we lost him already," Cam said slamming his hands on the steering wheel.

"Go up a couple more streets. If we don't see anything, turn around and we'll go the other direction.

Cam drove up two more streets to Maple Street and made a U-turn in the intersection. They looked up and down each street once more as they passed them again.

As they approached Lake Street on the return trip, Ben spotted a black Cadillac turning right off of Main onto Shore. "There he is!" he shouted, pointing his finger at Bob's car as it rounded the corner.

"Nice," Cam said.

The two men turned left onto Main and began their pursuit.

"Don't get too close," Ben advised.

"I know, I know. Just don't want to lose him again."

They drove along Shore Road for about a mile when they passed a sign that read; THANK YOU FOR VISITING DUNQUIN COVE. PLEASE COME AGAIN.

Ben looked at the clock on the dash board. *9:12*, He couldn't waste too much time, since he needed to be at school for Mica at two-thirty.

Bob sped up and so did Cam, as they passed a sign that said they were leaving the thirty-five mile per hour speed limit zone. As they rounded a corner, Ben looked out over the ocean.

"Soooo," Cam began. "Are you going to tell me about last night?"

Ben dropped his forehead against the door window with a thud. "What about last night?"

"What about last night?" Cam repeated. "Mildred said she caught the two of you in a lip lock."

"She did, did she?"

"She did. She ran right up those stairs and burst through the bedroom door and told me all about the two of you standing there arm in arm, the fire burning, the soft slow music playing, and the two of you playing a game of tonsil hockey."

"Glad to see she can keep a secret."

"The three fastest ways to spread news is telegraph, telephone, and tell-a-Mildred," Cam joked.

"Funny."

"So, what's next?"

"Well, I guess second base is next, Cam. What are we__, in high school? Christ! I don't know what's next.

"He's slowing down," Cam blurted out as he saw Bob's right side directional begin blinking and his brake lights brighten.

Ben pointed to a small dirt road ahead. "Pull in there, pull in there."

Cam quickly pulled to the shoulder and turned into a skinny dirt path. He brought the Buick to a stop behind a large cluster of button bush. The two men jumped from the car and ran, crouching, back to the edge of the road. Bob's car was nowhere in sight.

"It looked like he pulled off the road up a ways," Cam said.

"Let's go back down the path and circle around through the trees," Ben suggested.

They ran down the path for about twenty yards to a wooded area and then turned and made their way toward the area where they had last seen Bob's Cadillac. The trees ended at a small clearing. The ground was covered in dirt and gravel, and there were several sets of tire tracks. The clearing ran from the road to a bluff that overlooked the ocean a hundred or so feet below. Ben and Cam could hear the waves crashing against the large, jagged rocks below.

Bob's car sat in the middle of the clearing, parallel with the road, while he stood outside the car at the passenger side with his back to the water. He leaned against the car with his elbows above the door frame.

Ben and Cam squatted down behind their own tree watching intently.

"What's he doing?" Cam whispered.

"Who knows?" Ben shrugged.

There was the sound of and engine and Cam stated, "There's a car coming."

The car slowed and turned into the clearing, coming to a stop facing Bob's car ten feet away. Two dark-haired gentlemen wearing suits and sunglasses exited the car. Ben looked back at Bob and saw him put his hand in his coat pocket.

"Bob's got a gun in that right coat pocket," Ben said.

"How do you know that?" Cam asked.

"See the way that side of his jacket is hanging just a little bit lower? And when he reached into the pocket he wrapped his fingers around something. I'm guessing it's not a roll of quarters."

"That's close enough!" they heard Bob holler.

"We just want to talk," the driver said.

"I know how you guys talk, I've been doing your talking for you for fifteen years."

The passenger moved two steps toward Bob and started to reach inside his coat, under his arm. Bob quickly yanked his gun from his pocket and pointed it at the man.

"That's close enough," Bob yelled.

The man paused and pulled his arm back out of his coat and showed Bob his empty hand. "Take it easy, Bob."

Bob slowly made his way around the front of his car pointing his gun at the driver now. "Reach for your piece slowly and toss it into the dirt," he said.

The driver did as he was told. The Smith and Wesson 9mm hit the ground with a thud.

"Now you," Bob ordered, pointing his weapon at the passenger who reached into his coat and pulled out a revolver and tossed it into the dirt.

"Bob, this can only end one way," the driver warned.

"We'll see about that," Bob replied. "Now both of you get back in the car and toss the keys to me."

"You're only making things worse," said the passenger. "We just want to bring you back to Boston to talk to Vinnie."

"I think we both know how that ride would end. You think I don't know you sent someone up here to kill me already?"

"We're gonna bring *him* back too, Bob."

"He doesn't even know who he is!" Bob hollered. "Now get in the car; you're both lucky I don't kill you right here."

The two men opened the doors and climbed back in the car. The driver tossed the keys to Bob who caught them, turned and threw them over the cliff behind him.

Bob picked up both of their weapons and got back in his car, started the engine, and pulled around to the driver's side of the other car. "This was your one chance. We go way back and I don't want to, but if I see either one of you again I won't hesitate to kill you both. Now you go back and tell Vinnie that this is over, I'm done." Bob pointed his revolver out the window. "Do you understand?" Both men nodded, and Bob pointed his gun at the front tire and fired.

"Son of a bitch," the driver whispered as Bob pulled away and then he yelled, "Just because you want something to be over doesn't mean it's over. You owe him a lot of money, Bob."

Cam looked over at Ben. "Jesus! You're a hit man."

Ben shrugged his shoulders. "Sorry?"

"They sent you here to kill Bob."

"Yeah, that's what I got out of it too," Ben said with a heavy sigh.

"But why?"

"Let's get back to the house and find out."

As Ben and Cam turned to escape, Cam stepped on a branch. *Crack!* Ben put his finger to his lip. "*Shhh.*"

"Hey, there's someone in the trees," came a voice from behind them.

"Shit! They saw us. Run!" Cam exclaimed.

Ben took off running as Cam snagged his shirt on a branch. He grabbed the branch, trying to pull his shirt free. In a panic he began unbuttoning it.

"Hold it right there, grandpa."

Cam turned to see one of the men bent over with his pant leg pulled up, retrieving a revolver from a holster strapped to his leg. Cam turned and the branch came free. He rolled his eyes.

The other man walked toward them with a twelve-gauge shotgun in his hand. "Call your friend back here," he said.

"I don't think so," Cam replied.

"So that's how ya wanna do it." He looked to his partner. "Frankie, grab the old man and bring him over by the car."

"Sure thing, Tony," Frankie responded. "Come on, pops." He grabbed Cam by the arm and pulled him out of the trees and walked him to the car.

"Get on your knees," Tony commanded.

"Kiss my ass," Cam retorted.

Tony took the butt of his rifle and hit Cam behind the knee, sending him falling into the dirt as the palms of his hands hit the ground.

With his thumb, Frankie pulled back the hammer of his revolver and put it against the back of Cam's head. He turned back to the woods and yelled out, "I'm gonna count to ten, and if you're not standing right here in front of me, I'm going to put a bullet in this old man's head!"

Ben watched from the woods but didn't move.

"One … two … three …"

"Looks like your buddy isn't coming back," Frankie spat.

"Four … five … six …"

Cam, on all fours, stared into the dirt, thinking of Mildred. He wondered how long it would be before someone told her he was dead. He couldn't remember if he kissed her good-bye this morning. He wondered which one of their sons she would live with. "I'm sorry," he whispered.

"Seven … eight … nine …"

"Stop!"

Cam heard the click of the hammer as Tony gently released it and removed the gun barrel from his head.

Cam looked up to see Ben walking toward them. *Thank God*, he thought.

"Are you okay, Cam?" Ben called out.

"Don't worry about me, Ben."

"That's close enough, Max," Frankie hollered to Ben. "Make sure he doesn't have a weapon on him, Tony."

Tony hurried toward Ben. "Turn around, Max, and put your hands on your head." Keeping his gun in one hand and pointed at Ben, he frisked him with the other. "He's clean, Frankie." Tony turned and went back to Cam.

"Bob tells us you lost your memory," Frankie said.

"That's what happened," Ben said.

Cam started to stumble to his feet but Tony pushed him back to his knees. "No one told you to get up, ya old fart."

"So you don't remember me and Tony here," Frankie said, nodding his head toward Tony.

"Sorry, no."

"And you have no idea why Vinnie sent you up here?"

"No idea."

"I guess that's why Bob is still alive," Tony said with a chuckle.

"Well, Max, here's the thing," Frankie said. "Vinnie sent you up here to kill Bob,"

"Why would he want me to kill Bob?"

"Because that's what you do, Max__, you kill people," Tony answered.

"And we kill people too," Frankie said. "Ya see, when you disappeared Vinnie sent us up here to finish off Bob and then we were supposed to hunt you down and kill you."

"But now we don't have to," Tony said.

"You don't have to kill us?" Ben asked.

Frankie laughed. "Oh, yeah, we still have to kill you, it's just that, now, we don't have to hunt you down."

Tony laughed heartily. "Good one, Frankie."

Frankie turned his shotgun on Ben. "Turn around and walk toward the edge of the cliff, Max. Tony, bring the old man."

Tony grabbed Cam by the back of the shirt and dragged him toward the cliff.

Cam climbed to his feet and stood next to Ben, their backs to the water. "I guess following Bob was a stupid idea," Cam said.

"Everything is gonna be fine, Cam. Just remind me to pick up Mica at school after I kill these two gentlemen."

Frankie grinned and looked at Tony just as Ben shot forward, grabbing the barrel of Frankie's twelve-gauge and pointing it at Tony. Frankie instinctively pulled the trigger, removing most of Tony's head from his shoulders.

Without a moment's hesitation Ben grabbed the butt of the gun, driving it up into Frankie's jaw, and sending him stumbling backward to the ground.

Cam dropped to the ground and pulled Tony's revolver from his dead hand.

Meanwhile, Ben pointed the shotgun at Frankie.

Sidling up to Ben, Cam aimed the revolver at Frankie's head. "Call me old man one more time, you piece of shit."

Ben smiled. "I guess Tony was right__, Frankie, I do kill people."

"Wait, Max," Frankie said. "Please don't kill me; we go way back, Max, please. I got a wife … a kid."

Ben lowered his brow. "Do I have a wife or any kids?"

Frankie looked confused. "No … why?"

"Just wondered," Ben replied, then he put two slugs into Frankie's chest.

Ben and Cam loaded Tony and Frankie into the trunk of their car making sure to wipe away the finger prints from any places they may have touched. Then they changed the tire to make sure the car would roll easy. Ben took the butt of the shotgun and smashed the ignition switch, put the car in neutral, and together they pushed the car over the edge of the bluff. They stood and watched as the car bounced off the rocks below into the water and sunk below the lapping surface.

Cam smacked his hands together to knock off the dust and looked at Ben. "Does this make me a hit man too?"

"No."

"Do you want me to call you Max now?"

"No."

Chapter Twenty-Seven

Cam hung a right off of Shore Road onto Denton Street and pulled up to the curb. Ben looked up at the sign: Cargill Hardware and Rental. "They must have garage door springs here," he said hopefully.

Cam put the car in park and the two men climbed out and went in. A small brass bell over the door jingled and a heavy set blond woman behind a counter greeted them, "Good afternoon gentlemen."

"Good afternoon, ma'am," Cam replied as he stood in place and watched shoppers wander around the store.

"Can I help you find something?"

"Garage door springs," Ben said.

"Aisle five, right side, about halfway down."

"Thanks." Ben read the wooden signs that hung above each aisle and made his way toward the one marked five while Cam followed.

"Here they are," Ben said.

"Which one?"

"I don't know, they all look alike."

Cam pointed at a small spot of red paint at the end of one of the springs. "They appear to be color coded.

Ben grabbed a booklet that hung from a steel cable next to the springs and flipped through the pages. "Ya think that door is seven feet high?"

"Must be eight foot, since I'm six-two."

"How wide ya think it is?"

"Ten feet."

Ben ran his finger down the page until he came to the line marked ten foot wide, then ran his finger to the right till he came to eight feet tall. "Blue," he said.

Cam searched the rack. "They have every color but blue.

"Should we order one?"

Cam looked back at the woman behind the desk and noticed she was watching them with a big grin on her face.

"Can I help you with something?" she called out.

"We need a blue one."

The woman tapped at the keyboard next to the cash register and then said, "I'm gonna have to order one."

"We need two," Ben said.

"Then I'll order two."

Ben and Cam walked up to the counter. The woman slid a small pad in front of her and wrote down, *two blue springs.* "I'll have them Monday morning," she promised. "Can I have your name?"

"Ben ... Ben Dunning."

"Oh! Claire's brother-in-law. I heard you were in town. Fixing up the place are ya?"

"Just changing the springs."

"That's great. Claire could really use a man around that place. Ever since Clay … well you know … passed away. I mean, of course you know, he was your brother. I just meant …"

Ben smiled. "It's okay, I know what you meant."

"Your brother was a great guy. Everyone in town loved him; it was so sad when he passed."

"Thank you," Ben said. "I'll tell Claire you asked about her."

She slid the pad back over next to the register. "Okay then, I'll see you boys back here on Monday."

"Yes you will," Cam responded, and the bell rang once again as they walked out.

The car doors slammed shut and Ben checked the time. "To the school, Jeeves."

Cam started the car and put it in drive. "Which way?"

"Ugh!" Ben groaned. With brisk steps he headed back to the hardware store, alerting the lady at the counter when the bell overhead dinged.

"Forget something, honey?"

"Can you tell me how to get to the elementary school?"

She smiled and pointed up the street. "Up three blocks to Maple, take a right, the school is on the left."

"Thanks."

"Sure thing."

Ben climbed back into the car. "Up three blocks and take a right."

"Yes sir."

*****

Cam eased to the side of the street and parked across from the school as Ben swung open his door. "You want to come in with me?"

Cam pulled his cell phone from the center console. "No, you go ahead, I'll wait here. I want to give Mildred a call, tell her I love her."

"Yeah ... you should do that."

Ben looked up at the three story brick building as he walked up the sidewalk past the flag pole. When he went through the large glass double doors there was a sign on a thin chrome pole the read; VISITORS MUST SIGN IN. Underneath the instructions was a red arrow pointing to the left containing the word OFFICE, in white. He followed the sign to a door marked office and went in.

A woman with her black hair pulled tightly into a bun looked over her cat-eye glasses and sneered at Ben. "Can I help you?" Her voice sounded like the bad witch from *Wizard of Oz.*

"I'm here to pick up Mica Dunning."

"And who are *you*?"

"I'm his uncle, Ben Dunning."

"Do you have some identification?"

Ben pretended to search his pockets for an ID he knew he didn't have. "I ... uh, I must have left it back at the house."

A skinny woman in her early forties walked out from a doorway to the right. "Madge can you call Billy Fords parents and talk to them about the whole finger pulling, farting thing?" she asked.

When Madge pointed at Ben, the woman looked over and her pale face blushed. "Can I help you?"

Madge spoke quickly. "He says he's Mica Dunning's uncle, but he claims to have left his ID *back at the house*."

The woman gave Ben a big smile and moved toward him reaching out her hand. "You must be Ben," she said. "I'm Lori Callum, the principal here. Claire called me this morning and said you would be in to pick up Mica."

Ben took her hand and gave it a gentle shake. "I must have forgotten my wallet back at the house."

Madge still hadn't taken her eyes off of Ben.

"That's okay," Lori assured him. "Follow me, I'll walk you out back of the school, that's where they're working on the floats." She turned and walked out the door.

As Ben followed he looked back. "Thanks for your help, Madge," then he gave her a big smile. Madge didn't react, she just pushed her glasses up the bridge of her nose with her index finger and returned to her typing.

When Ben and Lori walked through the back door of the school, Ben could see Mica standing on the floor of the old wooden hay wagon, weaving brown tissue paper through a wall of chicken wire.

"Mica, your uncle is here," Lori said.

Mica's face lit up. "Ben," he called out. "I'm almost done."

"Looks great," Ben said.

Mica pointed to the top of a make shift mast sticking up from the middle of the wagon. "See the pirate flag?"

"Hey, that's awesome," Ben said, praising the waving skull and cross-bones.

Mica picked up more tissue paper and stuck it into the holes of the wire fencing as Ben walked around the float admiring the children's work. On the other side of the float three children sat on the ground using blue paper to hide the wheels to make the ship appear to be floating on water. When Ben returned to Mica's side of the float, Mica jumped to the ground. "We can go," he said.

"All done?"

"Yup."

"Let's go then. It was nice to meet you, Lori," Ben commented as he put his hand on Mica's shoulder and together the two of them walked back through the school.

Chapter Twenty-Eight

Cam gripped the steering wheel with one hand and in the other he held a waffle cone filled with two scoops of rocky road. Mica sat in the back seat licking a small vanilla with rainbow sprinkles and Ben did his best to suck a chocolate milk shake through a red and white bendy straw.

"I guess the extra thick shake was a mistake," Ben said, his face turning red while a large vein in his neck made a bulging appearance.

"Shoulda went with a cone," Cam informed him, taking another big lick.

"Yup," Mica agreed as the Buick swung into the driveway of the Colsome House Bed and Breakfast.

Cam came to a stop about four feet behind a blue Ford Taurus with New York plates. "Looks like we've got knew house mates," Cam said.

"Maybe," Ben answered warily. "Pop the trunk, Cam, and you and Mica wait in the car until I wave you in."

"What's up?" Cam asked.

"Just keep Mica in the car." Ben got out of the car and the trunk opened. He walked to the back of the car and looked inside at the shotgun and revolver. Picking up the revolver he released the cylinder and counted the shells__, six. He replaced the cylinder, stuck the gun in his waistband, and hid it under the tail of his shirt. Ben walked around to the driver's side window, leaned into Cam's ear and whispered. "If you hear anything you shouldn't, get that kid out of here and head to the police station."

Cam nodded and Ben disappeared through the back door. He looked down the cellar stairs, but the cellar lights were off. As silently as possible, he walked up the three steps to the kitchen__, no one. He looked left into the office and then tip-toed the length of the kitchen to the dining room door. He poked his head around the corner__, still no one in sight.

Ben took a deep breath, hunched over, and ran through the dining room to the hallway, where he could hear the television. George Gray was telling the next contestant to come on down. Ben peeked into the living room.

Mildred looked up from her knitting and furrowed her brow. "What are you doing?" she asked.

Ben straightened up and walked in. "Nothing."

"You feeling okay?"

"Yeah. Did new people check in?"

Yes, The Babbitts, about two hours ago."

Claire and Bob?"

"Claire is sitting on the front porch and I think Bob is up in his room."

"The new people up in their room?"

"No, they went for a walk about a half hour ago. Why all the questions?"

"I dunno, just wondering."

"Where is Cam?" Mildred asked.

"Waiting in the car."

"Waiting for what?"

"Um … nothing, I guess. I'll go get him," Ben answered, turned, and jogged back down the hall.

Mildred resumed knitting and shook her head. "Men."

Ben walked back to the car. "False alarm." He opened the back door and Mica got out and ran into the house.

"What now?" Cam asked.

"I say we head up to Bob's room and have a little talk with him."

Ben and Cam made their way up the stairs, down the hall, and stopped in front of Bob's door. Before entering Ben raised his hand, made a fist, paused for a second, and then knocked.

"Yes?" Bob called out.

"Can I come in, Bob?" Ben asked.

There was silence for a moment and then Bob answered, "Sure, come on in."

Ben walked in first and Cam followed. Bob sat on the edge of the bed facing the door, his left hand was in his lap and his right hand was on the bed underneath a pillow. "What can I do for you gentlemen?" he asked.

Cam closed the door behind him and Ben answered, "We just want to talk."

"About what?"

"Can you take your hand out from under the pillow, please, Bob?" Ben asked.

Bob looked Ben up and down and then concentrated on Cam. "Both of you turn around and face the door." They both did as they were told. "Now lift your shirts." They did and Bob saw the revolver. "Just wanted to talk, huh?" he asked.

"There was a car parked in the driveway; we didn't know what we would be walking into," Ben said.

"Take the gun out slowly, with your thumb and index finger, and toss it on the chair."

Ben did as he was told, turned back around and Bob slowly pulled his hand out from under the pillow. Ben slightly raised his hands. "We just want to talk," he repeated.

"About what?"

"We were at the bluff today," Ben said.

"We saw you there with those guys, Frankie … and Tony," Cam added.

"Jesus Christ!" Bob said. "Did they see you?"

Ben nodded. "Yes, they did."

Bob raised his eye brows. "And I'm guessing if you're still alive, that means they're not."

"You guessed right," Cam said.

"What did they tell you?"

They said I was hired to come up here and kill you."

"Did they say why?"

"No, Bob, so why don't you fill us in," Cam suggested.

Bob let out a long, drawn out sigh, rubbed his eyes with the palms of his hands and then ran his fingers through his diminishing black hair. "I'm not exactly a traveling salesman."

"No kidding," Cam said.

"Well not *just* a traveling salesman." Bob put his hands on his knees and pushed himself off of the bed and made his way to the one window in the room and looked out over the patio. "I used to be, but that was a long time ago." He turned around and looked at Ben and quietly asked, his voice calm, "Where do I start?"

"At the beginning," Ben answered.

"Like I told you yesterday, I lost my wife a few years back." Bob paused for a second and then resumed. "Well, things went bad after my wife was killed, I started drinking. I had always gambled a little bit, but after she died things got crazy. I barely remember those days, I was always drunk. I got in deep with a bookie, I couldn't pay, so he sent a couple guys to kick the shit out of me, and they did. Beat me bad. I was in the hospital for a week.

"When I got out of the hospital I was still broke, I had no way to pay this guy back, so I went to this loan shark someone had told me about and borrowed money. At first I made the payments, but after a while I got behind. The more I got behind, the more I owed. There was no end in sight."

Bob paced the floor a few times and then returned to the window. "One Saturday afternoon there was a knock at my door, and when I answered there were these two guys in suits standing there. One of them says, 'We need you to go for a ride with us.' I knew what that meant; it was the end for me. I get in the front seat with the driver and the other guy gets in the back. I remember smiling thinking, holy shit! I've seen this in a hundred movies. But they didn't kill me; they took me to a man named Vinnie Tartaglia. He was the loan shark I got the money from.

"Tartaglia says to me, 'Ya got one of two ways to leave this room, Bob__, walking across the rug or rolled up in one.' Then he explains to me what I have to do to pay off my debt and stay alive.

"Ya see, Tartaglia's men had high jacked a few trucks hauling prescription medication. A couple of them were on their way to Canada and a couple of them were headed for Mexico. He sat on these drugs for almost two years, until the heat died down, and now he was looking for a way to distribute them, without selling them on the street. Ya see, Tartaglia was just a shylock up until this point; he had never sold anything. He needed a salesman.

"So he comes up with this plan. I was supposed to use my connections and sell the medication to small pharmacies all over the east coast. I would sell and pick up the money, all cash, and someone else would deliver the drugs. I would jack up the price of the legitimate products I sold to them__, grab bars, toilet paper rollers, things like that__, to explain where the money was going. The pharmacies, in turn, would sell the drugs, and provide forged documentation, to nursing homes and small clinics. The clinics were getting their medication cheaper, the pharmacy was getting their medication cheaper. Everyone was making a profit and Tartaglia was making a fortune. It was win, win for everyone."

Ben furrowed his brow. "What if one of these pharmacies said no?"

Bob stared into Ben's eyes. "No one said no."

Ben and Cam exchanged a look. "What went wrong?" Cam asked.

"Before ya knew it, Tartaglia was buying stolen medication as fast as these scumbags could steal it, to keep up with the demand, twenty-five cents on the dollar. I finally told Tartaglia I wanted out. He said no, so I went on, business as usual, all the while trying to come up with a plan to get myself out."

"What did you do?" Ben asked.

"About a year ago I started skimming a little of the cash, not a lot, just enough to get me out and comfortable on an island somewhere."

"How much?" Cam asked.

"Eight hundred thousand dollars."

"Holy shit!" Cam said.

"How did he find out?" Ben asked.

"I have no idea. But about a week ago I went to this guy I knew__, he deals in fake identification, passports, birth certificates, things like that. I told him I needed the works, everything to start a new life. I didn't tell him why I needed it, but all I can figure is that somehow Tartaglia got wind of it."

"And now he wants you dead," Ben said matter-of-factly.

"And he wanted you to do it," Cam added, pointing at Ben.

"I wouldn't have even known if it wasn't for those two cops bringing me down to look at the photos of the two guys killed in that car accident. When I saw those pictures, I knew exactly what was going on."

"So, I work for this Vinnie Tartaglia character too?" Ben asked.

"No, not exactly. You're a freelancer, you'll work for anyone who can afford you. Vinnie has hired you a few times in the past, but we've never met, that's probably why he sent you. You still don't remember anything?"

"I'm starting to get bits and pieces. Everything is jumbled, nothing makes sense."

"Your name is Max Write, and other than what I've told you, I don't really know that much about you."

"How long before someone else comes looking for you?" Cam asked.

"Not long. Frankie was probably supposed to call in at a certain time. When they don't hear from him, they'll send a few guys. Tartaglia won't want me going to the feds, so he'll want to put a lid on all of this pretty fast."

"I'm sure they know where we are," Ben said. "Claire and the rest of these people aren't going to be safe here."

"We need a plan," Cam said.

Bob looked at the gun on the chair. "Were gonna be out gunned."

"There's also a shotgun in the trunk of my car," Cam said. "Of course, there's only three shells left in it."

Bob got down on his knee and reached under his mattress. "I've also got Tony and Frankie's automatics; there's fifteen rounds in each." He tossed the two weapons on the bed.

"Three guys, five guns__, they won't know what hit them," Ben assured them sarcastically.

Just then Bob's cell phone rang and he walked over to the dresser and picked it up. "Yeah," he said. "When? Shit … okay, thanks." Bob ended the call and stuck his phone in his front pocket.

"What's up?" Ben asked.

"That was a buddy of mine in Boston. Tartaglia's men left a half an hour ago, six of them in a black Grand Caravan."

Cam looked at his watch. "They'll be here in less than an hour."

Chapter Twenty-Nine

Cam kissed his wife good bye. "Sorry, Mildred, it's just something I gotta do."

"Cam, we should just call the cops and let them handle it," she urged.

"We can't call the cops; there would be too many questions, and Ben and Bob would probably be arrested. We have to end this today, Mildred."

"Too many questions?" she repeated. "You don't think there is going to be too many questions anyway?"

"They say they have a plan, so get in the car, go to The Cove, get something to eat, walk around town. Whatever you do, don't come back here till I call you."

Mildred put her hands on Cam's cheeks and kissed him once more. "Don't get yourself killed, you old fool," she pleaded as she climbed in the car.

"I love you Mildred," Cam said.

"I love you too." Mildred smiled, threw the Buick into reverse and backed out of the driveway as Claire helped navigate.

Ben and Bob watched from the front porch as they pulled away. Mica, on his knees in the backseat, waved out the rear window as, Ben sadly waved back and forced a grin. He had no idea what Claire thought of him and if she'd ever let him see Mica again ….

Cam joined Ben and Bob on the front porch and the three of them went inside.

*****

Cam watched through the living room window as a black mini-van pulled up across the street from the bed and breakfast, stopped, and cut the engine. Cam checked his watch. *Huh, two-thirty…, they made really good time*, he thought.

The driver's side and passenger's side doors opened in unison, and the side doors slid open a second later. Four men jumped from the side door, two with automatic weapons and two with semi-automatic hand guns. The driver and passenger got out, each carrying revolvers, and they all made their way toward the front of the house.

Cam left his look-out post at the window and walked down the hall to the dining room. The buffet had been turned over in the doorway and Cam knelt down behind it. He pumped the shotgun and aimed it at the front door. "Its show time!" he called out.

Someone outside yelled, "Johnny, you and Ricky go around that side; Chuck and Lane, down the driveway."

Seconds later the doorjamb splintered and the front door heaved violently open. The man in front took two steps through the door and Cam squeezed the trigger of the 12-gauge Winchester. He watched as the man's chest tore open, blood instantly bursting from the wound like a rose exploding from its bud, hurling him backwards into the man behind him. They stumbled, both falling to their backs on the front porch, the man in front lying atop the man in back.

The man on bottom struggled to free himself from under his dead partner while his pistol lay inches from his fingertips, just out of reach.

Cam put his left hand on the buffet, jumped over it, and aimed his weapon as he ran down the hall toward the front door.

As Cam reached the front porch, the goon made one last-ditch effort to reach his pistol. Just as he wrapped his fingers around the grip, Cam fired, his slug finding the man's forehead. His hand dropped to the porch, his death instant. Feeling his adrenaline pulsing, Cam turned and ran up the stairs.

Chuck and Lane heard the shots coming from inside the house. They looked at each other, turned, and ran back down the driveway toward the front of the house.

Johnny and Ricky also heard the shots but continued down their path, and across the patio. They stopped at the corner of the house. Johnny pointed at Ricky, then pointed at his own eyes, and then at the garage. Ricky nodded and stealthily stalked toward the garage. Johnny walked slowly across the back of the house, keeping as close to the wall as he could until he entered through the back door.

Cam slipped into Ben's room and ran to the window overlooking the backyard, knelt down, and looked out just as Ricky walked into the garage. The darkness of the garage lit up as Cam heard two gunshots. *Shit!,* he thought. *Bob's in there.* Seconds later he watched as Ricky stumbled out of the garage and fell face first into the driveway.

Bob walked out of the garage and looked down at Ricky, then up at Cam and nodded. Cam heard the back door swing open, then a gunshot. Bob spun around as Johnny's bullet grazed his shoulder. Bob pointed his weapon and fired, hitting Johnny in the right thigh.

Johnny limped across the driveway, aiming his pistol at Bob, and fired again, missing him. Bob pulled his trigger once more, but this time his gun jammed, so he turned and ran back into the garage as Johnny fired once more.

Cam took the butt of his shotgun and smashed out the window, hearing the shatter, Johnny turned on his bad leg and stumbled to the ground in the doorway of the garage. Laying on his back, Johnny fired once at Cam and then turned his weapon and pointed it into the garage.

Cam stuck the barrel of his gun out the window, aimed, and fired, hitting the two-by-four that had been holding up the garage door. At the sound of the creaking wheels, Johnny glanced up and screamed just as the door crushed his throat. His legs shook for a second and then all movement stopped. Satisfied, Cam turned and went toward the stairs.

Meanwhile, Chuck and Lane stepped over the lifeless bodies that lay on the front porch and cautiously went through the door. Lane's automatic was at his hip and Chuck pointed his pistol in front of him. The two of them made their way down the hall, climbing over the buffet, and into the dining room. They both turned toward the patio door as they saw Bob, outside, walking by, then he stooped over, his pistol in his hand.

Lane raised his weapon and aimed through the glass at Bob. "Looking for someone?" they heard behind them and spun around to see Ben standing in the office doorway holding a revolver in one hand and a semi-automatic in the other. Ben grinned as he watched their eyes widen twice their normal size and began pulling the triggers of both weapons.

Chuck fired twice into the floor as he staggered backwards and crashed through the dining room window, dead before he hit the ground.

Lane tried to aim his automatic, but emptied the clip into the ceiling as Ben fired several times into his chest. He stumbled back against the wall, his legs buckled under him and he hit the floor leaving a trail of blood on the wall behind him.

Ben walked slowly up to Chuck and stood over him. He watched Chucks chest slowly rise and then fall. He heard the gurgling as he fought to breathe. Chuck gazed up at the man standing above him and then closed his eyes tight. Ben fired into Chuck's forehead.

Bob came through the front door just as Cam got to the bottom of the stairs.

Ben leaned over and pulled Chuck's weapon from his hand and then felt around inside his jacket for another clip. Finding one, he ejected the clip that was in the gun and replaced it with the new one.

Bob and Cam walked into the dining room. Ben looked at Bob's shoulder. "You okay?"

"Just nicked me," Bob answered as he handed his pistol to Cam and took Lane's pistol and extra shells. "Let's go," he said as he went to the back door.

Ben turned to Cam. "You got everything here?"

"Yeah," Cam answered. "Go. Just be careful. Claire and Mica are going to be worried, so get back here as quick as you can."

Ben nodded and followed Bob out the door.

Chapter Thirty

Officer Marx stood with his hands resting on his gun belt as he stared at Cam. "So you're telling me that you were here watching television all by yourself when six armed gunmen burst through the front door and tried to rob the place?"

Cam sat on the front steps watching as they loaded the bodies into the three ambulances that sat parked in the street. "I almost can't believe it myself."

"And you shot and killed every one of them with their own weapons?"

"Well, luckily I got the jump on the first guy through__,"

"I know, you got the first guy through the door, got his weapon away from him, shot him, and the other guy. Do you really expect me to believe this story?"

"You believe what you want; I'm just telling you what happened." Cam looked up the street past the road-block and saw Mildred and Claire climbing out of the car and speed-walking down the street toward the bed and breakfast.

"Where are Claire's brother-in-law and that salesman?"

Cam gave the impression that he was deep in thought. "Ya know, I don't remember where they said they were going today."

Chet tried to intercept Claire as she and Mildred neared the house. "Claire, wait, it's pretty messed up in there."

She ignored him and side-stepped around him. "Cam is everything okay?"

"Everything is fine."

Mildred hurried to her husband and threw her arms around him. "Everything go as planned?" she whispered into his ear.

"Like a well-oiled machine," he answered.

Claire waited for Marx to walk away before asking, "Are Ben and Bob okay?"

"They're fine," he assured her, leaving out the part about Bob being shot in the shoulder.

"Where are they?" Claire asked.

"They went down to Boston to take care of something." Cam looked around. "Where is Mica?"

"He's with Lita. I didn't know what we would be coming home to."

Cam stood by as two paramedics wheeled a stretcher out of the house. He glanced down at the body bag as they wheeled it by and wondered which man was in it.

Amid the hustle of activity Claire approached Chet. "How long before I can get back in my house?"

"It's going to be a few hours, at least, Claire," he answered. He took Claire by the arm and led her away from the house. "Claire, what really happened here?"

"I don't know, Chet. Mica, Mildred, and I were getting something to eat at The Cove."

"Do you know where Bob Phillips and your brother-in-law are?"

"They said they had to run some errands today."

"Do you know when they will be back?"

"They didn't say."

"Okay," Chet said skeptically. He started to walk away and then turned back. "Claire, I did some checking, and I know your husband didn't have a brother."

"Well, he was *like* a brother, they were actually cousins."

"I can check into that too, Claire."

"I know you can, but please don't."

Chet smiled and walked away.

Claire heard a voice behind her. "Uh ... what's going on?"

Oh crap! The Babbitt's.

Chapter Thirty-One

Ben stared out the window across the Boston Common as Bob drove the Caddy down Tremont Street. Bob pointed up at a high-rise on the left. "He lives up there." Then he pointed into the park. "And he'll be taking his dog for a walk around five-thirty."

Bob took a right on to Stuart Street, a right on to Park Plaza, and then a right on Boylston Street. About half-way down the block he found a parking spot and nestled the car next to the curb.

Reaching across Ben, Bob opened the glove box and pulled out a long hunting knife, then slid the knife from its sheath and inspected the six-inch blade.

"A knife?" Ben asked.

Bob shoved the knife back into the sheath and stuck it in his waistband at the small of his back. "It's quiet."

The two men got out of the car and Bob went to a newspaper stand, put in some coins, and pulled out two papers, handing one of them to Ben. "Here, this is your disguise__, *man reading newspaper in the park.*"

"What are you going as?" Ben asked jokingly.

Bob folded his paper and tucked it under his arm. "The same as you."

They ran across the street and through the park until they came to a park bench that faced Tremont Street, directly across from Tartaglia's building.

Ben unfolded his newspaper and started skimming the headlines. Only a few minutes had gone by when Bob whispered, "Here he is."

Vinnie Tartaglia walked his miniature Yorkie across Tremont Street and down a path into the Commons. He whistled no particular tune, the pink leash in one hand and a plastic bag in the other. He walked past the concrete benches, the flag poles, and a hotdog vendor.

Bob got up first, followed by Ben and they began trailing him.

Near the frog pond Tartaglia left the path and walked into a group of trees to let his dog do its business. "Good girl," he said as he looked up into the trees for a bird he had just heard call out...

... And then the last thing he heard was Bob's voice in his ear. "There's only *one* way you're leaving this park, Vinnie, in a body bag." Bob wrapped his fingers around Tartaglia's mouth and plunged the knife into his back four times as fast as he could, moving the knife back and forth each time he drove it in. At the last plunge of the knife into flesh, he felt Tartaglia's body go limp. He let go of the knife, released his grip, and Tartaglia hit the ground.

Ben walked over and picked up the puppy. As the two men walked back across Boylston Street, Ben said, "So how do we get in touch with that friend of yours? It looks like me and this puppy are going to need to start a new life too."

Bob laughed as they climbed into the car. "I'll bring you there now," he said.

Chapter Thirty-Two

Claire stood at the corner of Shore Drive and Main Street watching the parade as it rounded the corner. She pushed up on her tip-toes to see if view could see Mica's float.

"He said he was after the fire trucks," Cam said loudly over the sound of the Dunquin Cove High School marching band.

"There it is!" Mildred cried out. "I can see the pirate flag."

Claire caught sight of it too. "Oh yeah," she said and waved. The lead fire truck sounded its siren and the crowd jumped. Claire scanned behind her and into the crowd several times hoping to see Ben, but didn't.

Mica's pirate ship drew closer and a hand came down gently on Claire's shoulder. "Did I miss him?" Ben asked.

Claire turned and looked up into Ben's eyes, "Ben!" she cried, and threw her arms around him and squeezed as hard as she could. "Thank God." Tears streamed down her face.

Ben tucked his hand under her chin, lifted her head, and kissed her. "Everything is going to be okay," he assured her.

"Mom," she heard Mica call out behind her. She turned and saw Mica at the wheel of the pirate ship, steering it down Shore Drive. She waved and Mica thumbs-upped her back.

"Ben!" he yelled. "Look, I'm driving the ship."

Ben waved. "Great job, buddy, great job!"

Cam slapped Ben on the back. "Get things taken care of in Boston?"

"Yeah. I don't think anyone will be bothering us again."

"And Bob?" Cam asked.

"He has a flight out of Montreal tomorrow morning for The Dominican Republic. By this time tomorrow he should be sipping Margaritas on the beach."

Cam looked back out at the parade. "Well good for him."

Ben wrapped his arms around Claire and together they watched the parade.

The End

Coming in Winter 2015

Ship of Fools
From the Tales of Dan Coast

ALSO BY RODNEY RIESEL

Sleeping Dogs Lie

From the Tales of Dan Coast

A mystery set in the Florida Keys follows Dan Coast, an unlicensed private detective of sorts, as he is hired to find the missing boyfriend of a woman who herself soon ends up missing. When someone from the woman's past unexpectedly shows up at Dan's home, with a story of faked deaths and missing life insurance money; Dan along with his sidekick Red set out to find the money, and the woman.

ISBN: 978-0-9883503-0-4

Ocean Floors

From the Tales of Dan Coast

The second installment in the Dan Coast series, Ocean Floors, is a tale of mystery and possible romance when a chance meeting with a beautiful young woman leads Dan and his trusted sidekick Red down a road of murder and kidnapping. Join Dan and Red as they try to solve the murder while searching for a missing friend.

ISBN: 978-0-9894877-0-2

Impaled

An Adirondack Short Story

Eric Stone is an investigator with The Town of Webb Police Department. Chuck Little is Head Ranger at the Nick's Lake campground. An unlikely duo, together they work to solve a murder that mimics a spree of gruesome murders taking place years earlier. Is it a copycat, or has the murderer resurfaced after all of these years? Join Stone and Little as they piece together the clues to solve this mystery taking place in the small village of Old Forge in the Adirondack Mountains.

North Murder Beach

A Jake Stellar Novel

The first installment of the story of North Myrtle Beach police detective, Jake Stellar. The spring bike rallies have ended, the spring breakers have all gone back to school, and the summer tourist season is a few weeks away. What better time for a police officer to take a nice quiet relaxing week off from work? That's what Jake Stellar had in mind. That is until someone from his past resurfaces to remind him of a terrible secret he has spent years trying to forget. In North Murder Beach, a story of revenge, Jake is unwillingly and violently forced to confront his secret from his past.

ISBN: 978-0-9894877-1-9

The Coast of Christmas Past

From the Tales of Dan Coast

Coast of Christmas Past is the third book in the Dan Coast series of books. Dan Coast is all set to spend Christmas just the same way he has every year for the past few years; alone and drunk. But when uninvited, unexpected guests arrive and throw a wrench into his holiday plans he is forced to sober up (slightly), and throw on a smile. Just when it seems nothing else could go wrong, a close friend is injured in what appears, to the police, to be a drug deal gone bad. Dan Coast and his sidekick, Red jump into action to find the truth while their friend lies unconscious in the hospital.

Made in the USA
San Bernardino, CA
26 February 2017